Racing the Moon

RACING THE MOON

By ALAN ARMSTRONG

Illustrated by TIM JESSELL

RANDOM HOUSE 🏠 NEW YORK

Text copyright © 2012 by Alan Armstrong
Jacket art and interior illustrations copyright © 2012 by Tim Jessell

All rights reserved. Published in the United States by Random House Children's Books, a division of Random House, Inc., New York.

Random House and the colophon are registered trademarks of Random House, Inc.

Visit us on the Web! randomhouse.com/kids

Educators and librarians, for a variety of teaching tools, visit us at RHTeachersLibrarians.com

Library of Congress Cataloging-in-Publication Data is available upon request.
ISBN 978-0-375-85889-5 (trade)—ISBN 978-0-375-95889-2 (lib. bdg.)—
ISBN 978-0-375-89309-4 (ebook)

Printed in the United States of America

10 9 8 7 6 5 4 3 2 1

First Edition

Random House Children's Books supports the First Amendment and celebrates the right to read.

She was quick and quicker to learn—
Bold and bolder to dare.. . . .

—Oregon legend
(adapted from Rudyard Kipling's *Kim*)

CONTENTS

for Zora

1

THE NEW NEIGHBOR

Early Sunday morning, Alex headed up the hill. The weight she was carrying was heavy on her shoulder, but she was unaware of it. "Hi, Amelia," she called to a blue dragonfly darting by. There were grass flowers in the warm breeze, a sweet scent that was almost dizzying. Then the sharp smell of fresh asphalt from the new road hit her with the thrill of a slap.

She stopped in front of one of the new houses. The ground around it was raw red clay. A large woman was on her knees, planting a bush. Her back was to the road.

"Hi!" the girl called as her dog's tail began waving in expectation.

No response.

She cleared her throat to get the woman's attention.

Nothing.

Finally Alex hollered, "Lady! Would you like to buy some plants?"

The dog barked, thinking it was some sort of game.

"Huh? What?" the woman called out, almost falling over as she jerked around, her trowel flying.

"Sorry," Alex muttered, starting to turn away. "I'm selling plants."

"Oh!" the woman exclaimed, her face clearing a little. "Well, hold on," she called in a friendlier voice as she stood up slowly like you'd fold out a pocketknife.

The woman was tall and square-shouldered, in jeans and a dark red shirt. She had dark curly hair and strong-looking hands. Her face was long. She looked like she'd been out in the sun a lot.

Alex was an eleven-year-old in a not-too-clean T-shirt and dirt-stained jeans. She'd just cut her hair herself for summer. The plants she was selling were in two baskets hung on the notched broomstick she carried across a shoulder like a coolie. The large brown dog wagged happily beside her.

The woman's face softened as she studied Alex. "Let's see what you've got. I like plants, and I sure do need *something* around here."

Alex figured the woman felt bad about getting angry. She pointed to her left basket. "These are azaleas, reds and whites," she said in a professional voice. "They're a dime each. In this other basket there's hollyhocks and foxgloves. They're two for a nickel. The foxgloves' official name is digitalis. You get heart medicine from the leaves."

The woman looked closely, then nodded. "Right! I'll take 'em all if you'll show me where they should go."

"Sure," said the girl as she lifted off her carrying pole and started emptying the baskets, delighted to have made such a big sale.

"First tell me your name," the woman said, wiping her big hands on her jeans. "Tell me about yourself and how you got into the plants business. Tell me inside. I haven't got my money on me. I've got milk, and I can give you a bomber bar I invented for the high-altitude pilots."

"A bomber bar? What's that?"

"Come on in; I'll show you."

Alex hesitated. She'd been warned about going alone into a stranger's house, but there was something intriguing about this woman. Alex imagined herself a spy, read all the spy stories in the magazines, figured she was pretty good at telling who was dangerous. She decided to risk it.

"Can Jeep come in too?" she asked. "He won't do anything."

She didn't say so, but Jeep was her protection. If she said "Sic!" he'd attack.

The woman understood. "OK."

"Got something for him?" Alex asked.

"I reckon," the woman said, smiling and sticking out her hand. "I'm Captain Ebbs. Call me Ebbs." She had a nice smile.

Alex rubbed her hand clean and shook Ebbs's. It was rough and twice as big as hers. Ebbs didn't paint her nails like Alex's mother did.

"I'm Alexis Hart," she said. "I live down the hill, last house above the creek. You can call me Alex."

Ebbs's house was a small white clapboard box like the others in the development, but inside it looked strange. The floors were bare and it was almost empty, except tacked to the walls were photographs of fighter planes, bombers, different-sized rockets, and a big balloon with a gondola underneath. In one corner there was a dark painting.

Alex stared at the photographs, the rockets especially. They were bigger, much bigger, than the ones in her book. Ebbs was in one picture standing with some officers and a tall man in a suit. She wore a military uniform with a narrow slant hat.

Alex's house was filled with rugs, stuffed chairs, and little tables with photographs of old people in polished silver frames.

"You waiting for the rest of your stuff?" she asked as

Ebbs pointed her to one of the two kitchen chairs and plunked down a glass of milk and a plate with a grainy-looking brown bar on it.

Ebbs shook her head. "Nope, this is it," she said, motioning around. "I move a lot because of my work, so I can't keep much, and anyway, things slow you down. Do you bicycle?"

"Sure," said Alex, taking a tentative bite of the bar, then putting it down. It tasted bitter.

Ebbs noticed but kept talking. "I sail a small boat. You don't want anything extra on a sailboat either. It took me a while, but now I live like I'm sailing, everything essential and shipshape. Do you like to sail?"

"Never done it."

"If you want, I'll teach you."

"Thanks," said Alex. Then she asked in a polite voice, "Is there a Mr. Ebbs?"

Ebbs's eyebrows went up a little. "My older brothers," she said. "But they don't live here. It's just me," she added quietly. "No family."

"Oh."

The dog whined.

"Right, I forgot!" Ebbs said. "Does he like cheese? I've got some old cheddar I can give him, but it's pretty hard."

"He'll eat *anything!*"

As Ebbs sat down with a yellow chunk in her hand, the dog waved his big forward-curling tail. He was short-haired but his tail was bushy. He came up to Ebbs slowly, stiff-legged and formal, sniffed, then took the cheese delicately and settled down to gnaw.

"Very dignified," Ebbs said. "What's his name again?"

"Jeep. He's my brother's dog, but he sticks with me." Alex paused, then added, "Folks usually want to know why he's called that."

Ebbs waited for her to say, but she didn't. Alex remembered her mother warning her about "going on," talking too much.

"So tell me," Ebbs demanded.

Alex relaxed. She liked to talk, and since Ebbs had bought her out, she didn't have to hurry on.

"Chuck named him that because he's the same color as his war surplus jeep," she began. "The garbageman found him hurt by the road and left him with us. He said he was a Chesapeake Bay retriever, but he hates water and he doesn't look like the ones in the book, so Mother says he's a mutt. He sleeps on my bed even though he's not supposed to. Mother says he makes my room smell like a caveman's cave because of what he rolls in. He rolls in *everything*!" She didn't tell how she pulled him close at night and buried her head in his chest, breathing in his damp warm dog scent.

Ebbs reached out and stroked the dog's head as he swished his tail slowly like a Chinese fan. "OK, Jeep," she said. "I've spent a lot of time in jeeps, so I won't forget your name."

As Jeep stretched out at her feet, Ebbs straightened up and turned to Alex. "So how did you get into the plants business?"

"It's my dad. We do it together. Most mornings he gets up at five, so I do too. I'm the only one because it's so early. He says dawn's the best part of the day."

"Right!" said Ebbs as she heaved up to get her purse out of the bread drawer. "What are you going to do with the money?" she asked as she counted out some coins.

"Buy stuff for *Moon Girl*. That's our rocket. We named it after this German rocket movie."

"No kidding!" Ebbs exclaimed. "What sort of rocket?"

"Like the ones in your pictures only a lot smaller," Alex said, getting up to study the picture of Ebbs standing beside the big rocket. "What do you do?"

"I work with our space scientists," Ebbs replied. "It's classified, so I can't say much, but in that one I'm with our top rocket engineer, Doctor Wernher von Braun. He's the one in the suit. I helped get him for us. His rockets like the V-2 we're standing beside are going to send us to the Moon."

"Doctor Von?" Alex asked, her eyes open wide. "The V-2 to the Moon? What do you mean, you *got* him?"

"Helped," Ebbs corrected. "He designed rockets the German Army used in the war. As it was ending, the Russians went after him for their program. We wanted him for ours. We got to him first."

"He worked for the German Army?" Alex asked, remembering newsreels of marching troops *Sieg Heil*ing Hitler and the swastika. "He was the enemy?"

Ebbs nodded. "Yes, but all he's ever *really* cared about is building rockets for space travel.

"Tell me about the rocket you're building."

"We made it to shoot up on steam," Alex said, "but when we got it going it fell over and chased us around. Then Chuck went away to school, but now he's back so we're going to fix it up to run on gunpowder."

"Gunpowder? You've got gunpowder?"

"No, but we're gonna make some. Our book's got the Chinese formula for it. Dad's got the sulfur we need—he uses it for killing bugs. The rest we'll buy at the hardware store."

Ebbs scowled. "A lot of people have got burned, lost hands and eyes trying to make gunpowder. Is your dad in on this?"

"No."

"I see," Ebbs said slowly. "How old is your brother?"

"Chuck's seventeen. He can make *anything,*" Alex said proudly. "Mother says he's got genius, but Dad says he's wasting it 'cause he can't buckle down and learn math. He was going to Tech, but he got kicked out."

"Uh-oh. Why?"

"'Cause he mixes things up when he reads, and nobody can read anything he writes. My other brother, John, says his writing looks like what ancient people did sticking sticks into mud pads, but I can read it and so can Rosy, the guy who's teaching us radio."

Alex went to another photograph, this one of a white and black balloon hung with ropes and sandbags. There were men in diving suits waving from the small gondola hanging below.

She pointed. "Is that like the balloons they send up to check the weather?"

"Yeah," said Ebbs, surprised, "only it's a lot bigger. It's called *Skyhook.* I work with it—send it way up with fruit flies and seeds to see how life does exposed to solar rays."

"Why?" Alex asked.

"Because I work on food for space pilots—stuff like that bomber bar you didn't like," Ebbs explained. "I made 'em for the crews of the bombers in the pictures over there—guys who'd be in the air six or seven hours on a run and needed something to keep their energy up so they'd be alert for the hardest part of the flight, the landing. I've invented other space food too."

Alex listened, rapt, for the next half hour as Ebbs described her concoctions and told Alex about the experiments they were doing to figure out how to keep the pilots from throwing up on liftoff and feeling nauseous in flight.

"Chuck and I read about space in the magazines," Alex said. "Are we going up soon?"

"Maybe," Ebbs replied, "but I can't talk about it. Tell me, though—you mentioned weather balloons. What do you know about 'em?"

"Nothing yet," Alex replied, "but Chuck and I are going to track one, find it coming down, and get its transmitter for our rocket."

"Right," Ebbs said, drawing out the word. "The same brother who makes the gunpowder—he's into radio too?"

"Oh yeah!" Alex exclaimed. "Saturday mornings we go down to the Radio Institute where Dad works. Rosy's teaching us. Chuck says we're going to build a radar dish to track *Moon Girl*."

Jeep started rattling his tags.

"We gotta go—Sunday dinner's at noon," Alex said, heading to the door.

"Come back later. Bring more plants," Ebbs called as Alex followed Jeep out.

"OK!"

2

TOMATO JUICE

Alex nodded to herself as she hurried down the hill sniffing the bands of honeysuckle fragrance that came in gentle waves on the warm breeze. "Rockets. Space food. Wait till Chuck hears," she muttered, quickening her step. "She said to come back." The dog wagged and trotted on ahead.

Chuck was Alex's main friend. She had other friends, but when Chuck was around she skipped them because his adventures were more interesting. He liked to show off for her. She knew he was dangerous. None of the neighbors let their kids play with him. Those that did often got hurt. Chuck got hurt a lot too, but he didn't seem to mind—it was like he wanted to go to the edge of everything.

"Dinner in ten minutes, dear," her mother called as

Alex walked into the house. Her mother was a small, quick, straight-standing figure. The gold chain with her heart pills capsule hung around her neck. Dinner smelled good. Pot roast.

Alex's mother kept their home as tidy as Ebbs's but with a lot more stuff, mostly old family things she'd brought back from Europe. She had gone to school in Germany and learned languages. Now she worked at home translating German songs. Alex liked to listen when her mother played the phonograph and sang the strange words.

Before Alex could eat she had to pass John's tests. It was part of his tutoring deal with their mother. Every Sunday noon before dinner Alex had to define and spell five vocabulary words and work some math problems from her schoolbook. She resented John's getting paid for ordering her around, but her grades *were* getting better. John said he was doing it so she wouldn't end up dumb like Chuck.

"In the development there's this lady named Ebbs," Alex announced as they sat down. "She's got pictures of airplanes and rockets all over her walls, says she makes food space pilots will eat—seaweed tubes they'll boil up into spaghetti and smear with chemicals—*if* they can swallow since they'll be eating upside down, and if their ears haven't blown out without pressure and gravity."

"Easy, Alley," Chuck said, laughing as his sister gobbled her dinner. "She's putting you on."

"No!" Alex exclaimed through a mouthful. "She told me a lot about her work, and she's got pictures. She's in one of them, in uniform with a bunch of men standing around this big rocket they captured. She says since a gallon of water weighs five pounds they can't take up much, so they're gonna drink recycled made out of their pee. . . ."

"Alexis! Please!" her mother said. "That's *vulgar.*"

Alex went on undaunted. "And before she started making the space pilots' food she made energy bars for bomber pilots. She gave me one. It's got coffee and raisins in it. She said she invented it for the long-distance pilots who'd be up in the air for hours and hours and had to stay sharp, but I had to spit it out."

John made a noise. Alex was delighted; she'd got to him. She was always fighting for a place in the conversation.

"Why she's telling *you* this stuff, I can't imagine," John said, "but if she's for real and you ever see her again find out why we want to go up there in the first place. It's empty! The stories we hear about looking for life? It's a boondoggle to get money for the airplane makers!"

"Empty?" Chuck said with a snort. "Some night pull your nose out of your books and look up!"

"Boys!" their mother said firmly. "Let's not argue about Alexis's new friend. I think it's nice that she's met someone in the development, and I'm sure Mrs. Ebbs is glad to have met someone from the *established* part of the neighborhood—"

"Ebbs is just Ebbs," Alex interrupted. "Or Captain Ebbs. There's no Mister around."

John rolled his eyes.

"That's not all," Alex said excitedly. "She told me how to train for taking off in spaceflight."

She leaned back in her chair and pantomimed. "See, you put a brick on your belly like this and push down real hard and grunt—*unnnnhhhh!*" she bellowed as loud as she could. Jeep lurched up with a woof.

"Alexis!" her mother scolded as Chuck laughed and her dad struggled to look serious.

"She got it from this German rocket scientist she helped capture—that and the experiment he did to see if our brains would turn to puddings on liftoff. He got some mice and tied them up in little hammocks and turned his bicycle upside down and fitted the hammocks around the rear wheel. He started cranking the pedals as hard as he could to get the wheel spinning fast enough to stress the mice like a pilot taking off, but he hadn't balanced them right, and one of the mice shot free and splattered against the wall and made a big mess."

"Alexis!" her mother exclaimed. "That's enough."

"Oh, it was OK, Mother. I mean, not for the mouse, but for the experiment. Ebbs said he got a fresh mouse, balanced the wheel more carefully, and started cranking again. When he stopped and checked, the mice were all alive, so Ebbs says that proves we can stay alive getting free of gravity. The guy she helped capture is named von Braun. She says he's gonna be the Christopher Columbus of space."

"A Nazi!" John snorted.

"Sounds like you've met someone really interesting," her dad said as John glowered.

"Yeah," said Alex. "She says she had to ride roller coasters a lot to learn what would keep the space pilots from puking in flight."

"Alexis!"

"It's tomato juice!" Alex giggled, getting up from the table to start clearing. "Tomato juice keeps you from puking."

3

SPACEMAN SMITH

It was Chuck's turn to wash. "A rinse will do for this one," he said, flipping a plate to John like it was one of their mother's phonograph records.

"Hey!" John yelped, almost losing it.

"Drop it, it's on you!" Chuck sang.

The next one he spun to his sister, but it was an easier pitch.

With John the washing was slow and exact; with Chuck it was a game.

When they finished Alex filled her baskets and headed back up the hill. Ebbs was out in her yard.

"Hi, Ebbs!" Alex called from a distance so she wouldn't scare her again. "I've got more plants."

"Great."

As they dug and planted Ebbs kept looking up to check the clouds.

"What are you looking for?" Alex asked.

"It's a habit from sailing," Ebbs explained. "Sailors are always checking the wind and clouds to get an idea what weather's coming. We're gonna get rain—that's what those wispy streaks overhead are telling us. I'll show you in my cloud book."

As they finished work and were rinsing their hands in the freezing hose water, Alex asked, "Now can I go in your house and look at those rocket pictures again?"

"Sure."

As Alex stood in the doorway, Ebbs went over to the photograph of the biggest rocket. "Here in this one I'm with that rocket engineer I told you about, Doctor Wernher von Braun. He says the first man to walk on the Moon is already alive: himself."

Alex studied the picture. "Chuck says we're going to walk on Mars. He says if you can see it, you can get to it. You think this Von guy's gonna go?"

"Maybe. What do they teach you about space in school?"

"Not much, but at home Chuck and I read about it in the science magazines Dad gets."

"Your dad's an engineer?" Ebbs asked.

"No. He's a writer. He works in a school for teaching people how to fix radios. They do it by mail—no classrooms or anything. He writes the ads and helps Rosy write the manuals and answer the students' letters. In trade for our mowing the lawn he's let us use the biggest tree in the yard for our Moon Station," she added slyly.

"Your *what*?" Ebbs exclaimed.

"Well, see," Alex said, "in one of the magazines there was this article about a space-exploring machine that went up on a rocket and then stayed out there. Dad helped us make one like what was in the picture with climbing boards going up the tree trunk like the ladder on the rocket in the *Woman in the Moon* movie, only I don't use it 'cause I can shinny up and down the escape rope faster than Chuck can climb. We crank Jeep up in a sling hoist, but he doesn't like being up there much."

"What do you do for food?" Ebbs asked. "That's my department."

"Apples and crackers. For cooking we rigged my magnifying glass so we can boil water, because you can't make a fire on the moon, you know—there's no oxygen."

Ebbs raised her eyebrows. "Crackers in zero gravity? Not allowed. You can't have loose stuff like cracker crumbs floating around the cabin. Particles would gum up the controls, get up your nose."

"Oh."

Ebbs went to get Alex a bomber bar. "Give it another try. It's gooey, so it doesn't crumble like crackers, and the taste does take some getting used to, but it'll give you a long burn of energy.

"So," Ebbs continued, "you and your brother are space explorers, right? Do you know about Captain John Smith?"

"The Jamestown and Pocahontas guy?" Alex asked as she pretended to nibble the bar while slipping chunks to Jeep.

"Yeah. I call him Uncle John because he's a relation way back. That's his portrait over there in the corner. He was a space explorer too, sailing out to the unknown in something like your Moon Station."

Alex walked over to look. Smith was a rough-looking man with a red beard. A long-haired boy about Alex's age stood beside him.

"Who's the kid?" she asked.

"His servant, T—that's all I can make out of his name. In the journal the rest is too smudged to make out. How old are you?"

"Eleven, almost twelve."

"Right," Ebbs mused. "Same age as Smith's T. At one point Smith traded him for one of Chief Powhatan's sons. After that there's nothing more about him in the journal."

"So he stayed?"

"More likely he died. Bad water. Anyway, I want to come see your Moon Station."

"Sure, but it's not all that much," said Alex. "John calls it Moonshine."

"Why? What's he interested in?"

"Government. Running stuff. He's the star. He wears a coat and tie to school every day because he's president of his class. He's fifteen. He gets prizes in Latin, so Mother pays him to tutor me."

"Huh," Ebbs muttered. "Well, I'd like to see what he calls Moonshine."

Alex headed home down the hill. *Spaceman Smith. Chuck will go for that. Smith and T are like Chuck and me.* She spat as she walked to get rid of the bomber bar's coffee taste.

4

THE RADIO TOWER

Tonight was John's turn to wash. Cleanup took a long time as Chuck juggled the pans and glasses to make John hurry up. "Come on, Alley," Chuck said when they finished putting away. "I'll take you for a ride."

He drove her and the dog over to the radio tower. "I've got to scale it to feel where the signal's coming from," he explained as he parked the jeep.

"Me too," Alex said. She was a good climber, fast but not as brave as Chuck—he'd tackle anything. People said he was a daredevil, crazy, no limit to what he'd try. Alex was always trying to keep up.

"No, Alley," Chuck said, handing her a camp stool and a blanket. "I need you to keep watch in case someone comes."

"Like who? What am I supposed to say?" Aside from

the tower's red lights glowing like slow heartbeats, every-thing else was dark and empty.

"I'm not expecting anybody," Chuck replied as he pulled on a pair of work gloves, "but if someone comes, tell 'em I'm a radio inspector checking on a weak signal. Here are the keys and my wallet. Scrape me up if I fall."

He scaled the fence like it was nothing. The cage around the ladder was locked, so he began pitching himself up the tower's struts like a squirrel jumping from branch to branch.

Chuck told her he was after something to do with radar, a special new kind of radio that would let him see things coming, like enemy aircraft, killer asteroids, infiltrators, spies.

Alex climbed trees to spy but mostly it was to imagine flying like the woman they'd read about in school, Amelia Earhart, who flew alone across the Atlantic. Alex liked it best when there was a wind; she'd hold tight to the pretend yoke in her flying tree, swaying high up like she was bucking a headwind. When there was no wind she'd sit so still in her tree perch that birds would come—jenny wrens singing busily in the understory, white-throated sparrows, cardinals, flickers, crows. Her father taught her how to make the birds' distress call—*pssht pssht pssht*—to get them to come close. "Birds are as nosy as people," her father said. "They'll always rush to the sound of trouble."

It was chilly. She wrapped herself tight in the blanket and got Jeep to snuggle up. She couldn't make out her brother anymore.

Twenty minutes later Chuck was swinging back down, black against the velvet sky, when Jeep began barking. A light was weaving jerkily up the alley. A policeman appeared. He fixed Jeep and Alex in the beam, then tried to catch Chuck, but wherever he aimed, Chuck had just left.

Jeep rumbled a deep growl.

"He's a radio engineer doing an inspection," Alex called, getting up.

"You keep hold of that dog and stay put!" the policeman ordered.

Flashing his light around, the officer yelled up at Chuck, "What the heck do you think you're doing?"

Chuck didn't reply until he'd dropped lightly to the ground and scrambled back over the fence. "Couldn't get to it. Too hot," he panted.

The policeman held his light on Chuck's face. Chuck didn't flinch or turn away. The light made his black eyes gleam.

"Get to what?" the cop demanded.

"Where the transmitter's beaming the signal," Chuck

explained, wiping sweat from his face. "It's weaker than it should be, so I was checking to see if something's blocking it—a fried squirrel, maybe—but it's too hot to get close enough to see."

"How old are you?" the policeman asked, taking out his notebook.

"Seventeen."

"You could kill yourself with a stunt like that!"

"So what?" Chuck said, not in a rude way but so honestly the officer blinked.

"Well, it made me sick seeing you up there," the man sputtered, "and it's trespassing, and what do you mean dragging this girl around?"

"I'm teaching her about radio," Chuck replied. "I'm a student of it. She is too. As for going up there to check, I'm not scared of heights. When I was little they held me by my heels upside down from the Empire State Building in New York, so I'm immune."

The officer's mouth formed an O. "Your parents did *what*?"

"They're not my real parents," Chuck said. "I'm an orphan."

Alex pinched her lips together. Chuck's face turned deep rose under his dark skin as he talked excitedly. Alex knew his stories. She figured he was trying on different lives to see what fit.

"And this one," the officer said, pointing at Alex. "She's an orphan too?"

"No. Her mother's sick. I'm taking care of her."

"I'm taking you home to your dad," the officer said.

"Stuart's not my dad."

"Who is Stuart?"

Chuck pointed to Alex. "Her father."

The police car followed them home, the headlights on high bathing them in cold light.

Alex's dad, a strong, ruddy-cheeked man, was waiting at the door. Alex looked like him.

"You Stuart?" the policeman asked.

The man nodded.

"I caught him climbing the radio tower!" the policeman said loudly, indicating Chuck. Stuart put his finger to his lips and pointed upstairs. The policeman continued in a whisper.

"He said he was checking where the broadcast came from, but he's just a boy so he can't be an engineer or anything, and what's he doing dragging this girl around?"

Stuart frowned and nodded slowly.

"He says he's an orphan," the officer went on. "He says you used to hang him by his heels from high buildings so heights don't bother him."

"I'll take care of it," Stuart said finally in a quiet voice.

"What about the orphan and the hanging stuff?"

"He's our son, and I never hung him from anything," Stuart said. "So now, officer, it's late, and you've got other things to do. I appreciate your help. I'll take it from here."

With that, he eased the man out.

Chuck started talking fast as the door shut. "I wanted to see if I could feel the broadcast. Rosy says it's like a pulse, but all I felt was heat—no pulse at all. . . ."

His dad shut him up with a wave of his hand. "Tomorrow's a school day," he said angrily. "Alex should be in bed. Worse, you gave Mother a scare. She went up to tuck Alex in. No note or anything! I went out to the Moon Station to look for her. When I told Mother I couldn't find her, she had an attack. Had to take a pill."

"Oh jeez," Chuck said with a sigh. "I'm sorry."

Alex wasn't surprised that her dad didn't say much to the officer or to Chuck. He wasn't a talker, but Alex could tell he was upset about Chuck's getting caught. It wasn't the first time, but her dad didn't have any control over Chuck. Nobody did.

5

Looking for Aliens

Early morning a week later, Chuck came into Alex's room bent under the heavy Signal Corps field radio strapped to his back. He was carrying a telescope.

"Come on," he said. "It's almost time. At the observatory the other day the navy guy in charge told me they launch the weather balloons at dawn. Looks like a storm's coming, so maybe we'll catch its signal, maybe even see it."

He led them downstairs past their parents' room and their mother's workroom, Jeep following wagging hopefully.

"Take this and look over there," Chuck ordered, handing Alex the telescope when they got out in the yard. "Toward DC. What you're looking for is a black rubber balloon with a basket hanging at the bottom. That's where the weather sensors and transmitter are."

Chuck kept talking as he slipped the radio off his back and knelt down to work it. "The navy guy let me look at the transmitter even though it's secret because I told him I was studying radio. It's really small—half the size of a toaster. I even got the frequency it broadcasts at."

Alex aimed where Chuck had pointed. There was a steady breeze. The leaves sounded like waves. All she could see were swells of low gray clouds. "Cumulonimbus," she muttered. She'd been looking in Ebbs's cloud book. "Storm clouds."

Jeep looked up briefly, then yawned a long, wide-open moan of boredom.

Chuck had on the headphones and was adjusting the radio's controls. He'd just said, "No signal yet," when there was a rumble of thunder.

The dog started up whining and rattling his tags. He hated thunderstorms. Alex did too. She felt the down on her arms rise—a warning of electricity in the air, her father said. Chuck took off the headphones and began snapping up the radio's cover. "Missed it. Too much static."

"What if the balloon gets caught in the storm?" Alex asked. "Will the lightning blow it up?"

Chuck shook his head. "No. It's not grounded, so the charge will just pass through it like it does with an airplane," he said as he hoisted the radio onto his back, "but watch out if you're on the pot in a thunderstorm. I heard about a guy who got zapped; bolt shot right up through the toilet—water's a ground, you know—scorched his butt."

"You gotta be kidding," Alex said, but there was no reading Chuck's face.

"See you after school," he said, turning away. "I'm going over to the airport to watch the flying lessons, maybe get the instructor to give me a ride once the storm passes.

"Oh, wait," he called as he struggled to shift the radio so he could fish some paper and a small screwdriver from his pocket. "I got this out of the latest *Popular Science.* The microphone they're using at school for announcements—it still looks like this one?"

Alex studied the picture. "I guess."

"Good. This is all you'll need. After school, go to the assembly room and unscrew the microphone's back. You'll see two wires, a red and a black. Switch 'em like it shows in the picture, then screw the back on again."

"What'll happen?" Alex demanded.

"You'll see tomorrow morning. Just make sure you bring back my screwdriver."

*   *   *

As she walked to school Alex weighed Chuck's dare. There'd been some she'd balked at, especially the stealing ones, but she was curious about the microphone. Nobody could do tricks with radios like Chuck.

She sweated as she hung around after school until the hall was clear. She sneaked into the assembly room. Her hands trembled as she switched the wires.

On her way home Jeep met her at the creek bridge as he always did, smiling his toothy, lips-pulled-back grin, snuffling, whimpering, snorting, his body wriggling with delight, his whole being asking *Where have you been?*

She potted up some more plants. When she figured Ebbs would be home from work she and Jeep went back up the hill. The plants were just an excuse. She wanted to get some arguments to use against John.

"My other brother says there's nothing in space for us to bother with," Alex said as they worked. "But Chuck thinks there's life. That's what he wants radar for—to watch for space aliens. You think they're out there?"

"We have to go to find out," Ebbs said. "But whether we find life or not, soon we'll be creating it out there on our own with those seeds I'm working with, planting colonies in space like Captain John Smith did here.

"Looking for life in space is tricky," she continued, "but there's no trick to finding space rocks, which is something else I'm interested in."

"Space rocks?" Alex asked.

"Right. Ever seen one?"

Alex shook her head. "No. I collect rocks, though, crystals."

Back inside Ebbs went over to the piled-up card table she used as her desk. She felt around at the bottom for a moment, knocking something off the top—a snapshot of a man with his arm around Ebbs's waist. Ebbs picked it up, then handed Alex a shiny black square the size of a stamp.

"These small ones are called meteorites," she said. "It would have gone through you like a white-hot bullet had you been standing in Australia where it crashed."

Alex juggled it like it was still hot.

"Take it for luck," Ebbs said. "It's older than the sun."

"Don't you want it?"

"Of course I do! That's why I kept it, why I'm offering it to you. You don't want to make a gift of something you wouldn't want to keep yourself, right?"

"Yeah, OK," Alex said, embarrassed because she never gave away things she liked. "It really came from space?"

"Yup, one of the thousands that hit Earth every year."

"What if . . . ?" Alex started to say.

Ebbs shook her head. "Don't worry. Since most of

Earth is covered with water most of them land in the ocean, and that may be how life got started here, some bit of life-bearing space matter fell into the ocean and got us going, right down to the bit of celestial fire that burns in you."

"What celestial fire burns in *me*?" Alex asked.

"The fire that makes your heart beat and your little finger go up and down," Ebbs explained, moving hers. "Some scientists think our life-bearing rocks came from Mars. They think there was life there once, but then a massive asteroid wiped it out, sending a chunk of spore-bearing Mars rock to us like Noah's ark."

Alex was worried. "What do we do if we see something like that heading to Earth?"

"Right!" said Ebbs. "You see little ones burning themselves up all the time—shooting stars, comets, meteor showers. But a big one? An asteroid? Right now we can do nothing, and that's where our project comes in. In outer space they travel slowly. They only pick up speed when they get close enough for Earth's gravity to pull them in. The new radar dishes like the ones we're testing on Wallops Island will help us spot something threatening when it's still far away. Then with one of Doctor von Braun's new rockets we'll be able to blow it up or maybe nudge it back out into space, seeded with the stuff I'm working on—make it into a space farm."

"Neat!" Alex said.

"Hey! That's nothing compared to our *big* plan!"

"What's that?" Alex asked.

"A big-enough asteroid could become our first space colony. That's what we're getting ready for—a place for you and Chuck to stop on your way to investigate life on another planet."

"Mars," Alex said. "We're going to Mars."

6

HYBRIDS

That night in the Moon Station's cockpit Alex cranked the hand generator. Red lights glowed over switches and dials, the pretend radar gave off a pale green light, the big vacuum tubes glowed pink with what looked like tiny buildings inside. Chuck was navigating. Suddenly he called to Alex, "Pilot to copilot: sighting craft approaching fast fifteen degrees off starboard." It was the flashing lights from the WTOP radio tower. "Adjust thrust," he ordered as Alex turned valves. "Quick, signal identity and greeting in Code Alpha."

"Roger," Alex snapped in her official voice as she cranked the generator with one hand and tapped out a message on the Morse code key. She looked out of the Station's nose cone. The red and green signal lights were pulsing as she tapped *dot dash dot dot dot dash dash.*

"Message received," Chuck announced. "Prepare to dock. Mission done."

They leaned back for their evening chat.

"Sounds like huffduff to me," Chuck said when Alex told him about Ebbs's space colony plan.

"It isn't. Ebbs says she knows the people who build rockets and she's been to some island near here where they track asteroids on radar."

"Wallops?" Chuck asked, sitting up. "She knows about the radar dishes on Wallops?"

"Yeah. That's it. Wallops."

"Huh!" said Chuck. "If she's for real she must have a really high security clearance. What I don't get, though, is why she's got all this time for you."

"Dad says it's the plants. He says working with plants you make friends and it doesn't matter how old you are or if you're man or woman. Anyway, do we ever hear voices from space?"

"Maybe in some of the static we get on the radio," Chuck replied. "Rosy says the new radar is going to pinpoint where it's coming from. That's why I want to get in on it, and it sounds like maybe you've met somebody who can help me."

"I guess," Alex muttered. She'd told herself she wasn't going to tell Chuck much about Ebbs because Ebbs was *her* find, and if Ebbs met Chuck, maybe she wouldn't pay attention to her anymore, and maybe Chuck wouldn't either. Alex had always felt possessive about Chuck, and now she felt possessive about Ebbs too. "Because they're *interesting,*" she told herself. "They're *hybrids.*" That was the word her dad used to describe his rarest plants.

Later, in her bedroom, Alex felt for the space rock in her pocket. She hadn't shown it to Chuck because it was private, a symbol of her special bond with Ebbs—Ebbs had given her something she'd prized. Alex had gotten lots of presents, but they'd all been bought things or hand-me-downs, nothing the giver really wanted to keep.

Alex's room was in the front of the house. Her shelves were filled with books, stuffed animals, junk, her box of crystals. A large chunk of petrified wood was on the corner of the lowest shelf. Every night she saw a head in the shadow where streetlight hit it. She knew she was too old to take it for real or be scared of it, but she was, so every night she'd bargain with the shadow to leave her alone.

Tonight she didn't notice the head. She watched the sky for space rocks. Suddenly a bright greenish light flashed through the stars. She held her breath and felt for the smooth square she'd put under her pillow. *Ebbs said it was going more than a hundred feet a second. What if there's some kid standing outside in Australia?*

She watched the sky. There were no more shooting stars. She looked around her room. It was as if she were seeing it for the first time. She got up and took down the pictures of the dancing insect musicians. When she got back in bed she stared at her shelves. "Ebbs doesn't keep things she isn't using," she murmured, getting up again.

Jeep lay on the bed watching as Alex cleared her shelves until the only things left were *The Greek Myths* and the crystals. *"Shipshape"—that's what Ebbs would say. "Just the essentials and everything shipshape."*

A painting of Icarus was on the book's cover. As Alex stared, the sun melted his wings of gold, the feathers went free, Icarus fell horror-stricken toward the blue-green sea. She heard his cry, but his father was out of sight and the ship in the distance was too far away to help—even if the sailors *had* seen something amazing, a winged boy falling out of the sky.

Just then Jeep shot under the bed like a mole to his hole. Alex's mother was coming up the stairs. "Time to tuck in, dear," she said, breathing hard as Alex slid under the covers. If her mother noticed anything changed, she didn't say. She didn't come up often—only when she felt strong enough to give her daughter a good-night kiss. Tonight, though, was different. She had something on her mind.

"You're almost twelve, Alexis," she said as she sat down on the bed, "so I think it's time you spent less time in that Moon Station and quit climbing up trees where nobody can see you, coming home scratched and bruised. And your hair," she continued as she smoothed what was left of it, "your lovely hair all chopped away. Oh my."

Alex gently pushed her mother's hand away. She felt a cautious tenderness for her, as if her mother were a delicate china cup.

"It's time for you to act more ladylike, Alexis, pay more attention to your schoolwork, start music lessons, and dress more carefully. Skirts. The neighbors say you're becoming a tomboy."

"I'm *not*," Alex protested, "but I don't want to do that other stuff. I want to learn radio and flying and do space work."

"No, Alexis," her mother said. "What you're talking about is not for girls."

Alex lurched away. "What do you mean? Mrs. King had us read about this woman who flew alone across the Atlantic. They called Earhart a tomboy too, but she wasn't. Ebbs says all kinds of women are pilots now. She says the first space pilots will be women because they weigh less. Chuck and I are going to do it together."

Her mother got up wearily, shaking her head. "Charles," she corrected. "His proper name is Charles." She bent over and kissed Alex on the top of her head. "Good night, dear. That woman pilot you're reading about crashed somewhere in the Pacific. We don't want that to happen to you."

7

PEPSI-COLA HITS THE SPOT

As soon as Alex's mother went downstairs, Chuck knocked on the door. He'd been waiting.

"Come on," he called softly. "I need your help. We're going to go fix Reggie with some sugar water."

Right off Alex knew what was up: it was in the magazine story they'd just read about some Dutch kids sabotaging a German patrol car during the war. They'd poured beet syrup into the gas tank. It gummed up the engine like burning sugar in a kitchen pan.

The night before, Reggie had taken the girl Chuck liked to a drive-in movie in his father's new car. Going out in a car had to beat bouncing around in Chuck's war surplus jeep. Besides, you could be private in a car; the jeep was all open.

"I've made the mixture," Chuck said, holding up

a bottle. "I need you to hold the funnel while I pour it in."

Lucky for Reggie the garage was locked.

"Tomorrow," Chuck growled. "I'll jimmy the lock."

The next morning Alex waited uneasily in the assembly room for Mrs. King to come in for the Pledge of Allegiance. She chewed her lips and didn't join in the usual chatter. She pictured sparks, a big flash. People had gotten hurt with some of Chuck's tricks.

The room was buzzing like a swarm of excited bees when Mrs. King strode in and lifted the microphone from its stand. She pushed the switch. "Pepsi-Cola hits the spot!" blared out in a high tinny voice as

Mrs. King screamed and dropped the instrument. It crashed, but the singing and talking kept going until she pulled the connection from the wall. She was pale. "Dismissed," she whispered to the gaping crowd. "Dismissed to class."

"Did it work?" Chuck asked when Alex got home.

"Yeah, perfect," Alex said. She didn't let on how nervous she'd been. Chuck would have teased her for being sissy. "Tell me what you did," she said in her cool scientific voice.

"It's what *you* did. Switching those wires turned the mike into a little radio. It doesn't take much. Remember the crystal set? I heard about a woman who got signals through the silver fillings in her teeth, thought she was crazy hearing voices all the time, so they took out her fillings and it stopped."

"You gotta be kidding," Alex said.

"I'm not. She got false teeth, but then she complained they hurt, and besides it was suddenly too quiet in her head, so she said she wanted her little radios back."

Alex shook her head and changed the subject. "Did you get a flying lesson?" she asked, imagining herself Amelia Earhart at the stick.

"No, not yet, but I watched what the instructor and the student were doing. It's a Piper Cub with a

45

beauty of an engine, no muffler or anything so you really hear it. There's not a lot of controls to work it with either, and you know what? There's no key or lock— you just open up the throttle a little, turn the prop slowly a couple of times to prime it, turn on the ignition, then flip the prop hard to get her started, hop in, take off."

He smiled at Alex the way he always did when he dared her. "Think you're up for some prop flipping?"

"You gotta be kidding," she said again, turning away. *But what if he was flipping the Airster's prop for me?*

She went out and worked in her garden for a while, tilling and weeding as she thought about flying. A monarch butterfly coasted by, then another. Alex was delighted. Her father had pointed out their gold-dotted, bright green cocoons hanging like peanuts under the porch railing. "Hello," she said softly.

Alex dug up some special plants for Ebbs. She loaded her baskets and headed up the hill.

"Right!" Ebbs called out when Alex knocked. "Just got home myself. And you brought more plants? Good."

"These aren't to sell," Alex said. "They're my thank-you for the space rock. They're cuttings from a wild azalea I found."

Ebbs looked at her, expecting her to say something more. After a pause she said "Nice" as she lifted out the plants. "When we get back inside I want to hear about that rocket you're building."

Alex told how they'd made cherry bomb bazookas until one of them blew up and Chuck got hurt.

"Good Lord!" Ebbs muttered, pointing Alex to the kitchen chair as she got out graham crackers.

"He tells people he got the scar on his face in a knife fight with some spies," Alex said, "but it was really the bazooka. He told Dad he got it doing a bike trick, but Dad must have found out because all the pipes and cherry bombs disappeared."

"So now you're building a real rocket," Ebbs said. "How'd you get into that?"

"It was Mrs. Knapp, the town librarian," Alex explained. "She knows what we're interested in. She got us the new history of rockets book with pictures and the formula for gunpowder. *Moon Girl* looks like the Chinese rocket in the book, but it's a toy compared to what's in your pictures."

"Size doesn't matter," Ebbs said. "What von Braun started with looked like toys too, but they were the real thing. Go on."

"It started out as the steam one pictured in the book,"

Alex said, "but it didn't go up, it just flopped over steaming like mad, whistling and chasing us around like it could see us. It scared Jeep so bad that when we get it out now he goes under the porch."

Ebbs snorted. "Then what?"

"Like I told you," Alex said, "next time we're going to pack *Moon Girl*'s shell with gunpowder like it shows in the book."

"Yeah," Ebbs muttered, "but can it take the shock? What's it made of? What materials? That's what VB would want to know."

"Copper," Alex said. "It's an old fire extinguisher we turned upside down and made a pointed nose and fins for."

She started to explain how it was supposed to work, but Ebbs was after something else.

"Where'd you get it?" she demanded. "VB says the hardest part of his job is getting parts. Where'd you get the extinguisher?"

"Hector's junkyard on Seventh Avenue," Alex explained. "We go there with metal we've collected—aluminum, brass, copper. We trade him for parts for the Moon Station and for our inventions. He got us the Plexiglas when we told him the Moon Station needed a nose window like bombers have."

Alex hesitated. Suddenly she felt uncomfortable about what she was about to say.

"And?"

"W-well, uh, see," Alex stammered, twisting her feet under the chair, "Hector'd always let us take what we needed. He'd pay himself back the next time we came in with the metal, but this time he said no because the fire extinguisher was an antique he could sell for more than its scrap value. He wanted five dollars for it."

Alex hesitated again.

"And?" Ebbs prodded.

"We didn't have any money, so Hector asked Chuck what we had at home for trade. They had a talk and Hector said he'd hold it for us a couple of days."

Alex stopped talking.

"So what'd you take him?"

"Spoons," Alex mumbled. "Mother's got a bunch she never uses. They were in the attic."

Ebbs stared at her, eyes blazing. "You didn't ask, you just took? That's stealing."

Alex looked away, her face getting hot. She felt bad that her new friend saw her as a thief. She hadn't thought of herself like that before. When she and Chuck stole things—mostly from stores—he'd always used a fancy name for what they were doing: "liberating." That made it sound like they were simply putting things where they belonged.

"Bring Chuck up here," Ebbs ordered. "I want to meet him."

8

AIR HART

On Saturday morning Alex's dad got her up early. She'd forgotten—she thought it was to do plants, but they were all in the kitchen waiting for her.

"Twelve!" her mother announced when Alex appeared. She'd circled Alex's place at the table with flowers and strawberries. There was a honey cake stuck with twelve candles, and there were cards—one from John with two dollars of his tutoring money—and a small box Chuck must have wrapped. She looked for something from her parents but there wasn't anything until "Zoom!" her dad called out, buzzing Alex with a bright yellow model biplane. He spun the prop as he landed it at Alex's place.

"It's Amelia's plane!" she cried.

"You bet, just like in the photograph—Aerospace

51

model nine Merrill-type. Made it myself down at the Institute—with Rosy's help."

"Quick, open my present!" Chuck exclaimed. "And I didn't know about the plane!" He had made Alex a pair of flying goggles—big rounds of tinted glass molded into what looked like a bathing cap. AIR HART was written across the top in Chuck's blocky letters. "I read about

her," Chuck said. "I bet she crashed because her radio broke, or she didn't know how to work it."

Because it was her birthday Alex was excused from cleaning up, but she helped anyway. "Now we gotta go to Ebbs's," she told Chuck. "I promised I'd bring you up."

Ebbs must have seen them coming. Before they could knock she opened the door, smiling and holding out her hand.

"Like a spider lying in wait," Chuck muttered as Ebbs exclaimed, "Come in! You're Chuck, right? The Moon Station, weather balloons, steam rockets, and radar brother?"

"Yeess," said Chuck slowly, giving Alex a surprised glance.

"Good!" Ebbs said. "I want to come see your Moon Station."

"You can come right now."

Ebbs shook her head. "First things first. Have you made the gunpowder yet?"

"No," said Chuck, frowning. "The sulfur's gone. Stuart must have used it up."

A flicker crossed Ebbs's face.

"Right!" she said, drawing out the word the way she did. "Next question: can you swim?"

"Yes," Chuck replied, squinting at her, trying to figure out what she was up to.

Ebbs turned to Alex. "How about you?"

"Sure."

"Good," said Ebbs. "I've got lemonade. Sit down."

Alex took her regular chair.

As Ebbs poured the glasses, Jeep started rattling his dog jewelry.

"Right, Jeep. More cheese?"

The dog ducked his head and licked his chops.

"So," Ebbs announced once she'd taken care of the dog and handed Chuck a bomber bar and given some graham crackers to Alex. "Since you both can swim, I want you to help me take a space trip."

Chuck's eyebrows went up.

"Here's the proposition," she said. "I've got a sailboat and I need crew. You guys go out cruising in the Moon Station all the time, so here's your chance to go out like you're really in space—stars, Moon, planets overhead, dark depths below, no land in sight. Save for the water noise it's just as silent as if you were a thousand miles up, and it's every bit as dangerous because you can drown in space just like you can drown in water—lack of oxygen, right? It'll get you ready for your Mars trip.

"I can sail it alone," she continued, "but *No Name* was built to carry a crew of three, and since I'm new around here I don't have any sailing buddies yet so I'm hoping I can enlist you. It'll be a paying job. I want to sail down the Potomac and out to Tangier Island, where I've got an old army buddy."

Chuck looked at Alex. "We don't know about sailing, but I'm willing to try if Alex is."

Alex nodded. "Sure, but that's a funny name—*No Name*. How come you call it that?"

Ebbs leaned against the doorjamb. "For a few weeks during the war I was a CIC agent, Counter Intelligence Corps. Like I told Alex, as things were winding down in Europe, because I knew about nutrition I was sent to help feed the refugees, but going over I ran into the officer who'd been in charge of my high-altitude bomber work. He got my orders changed, got me assigned to help his team collect dope about the Germans' V-2 missiles and to find Doctor von Braun himself because he and his rocket team were way ahead of everybody."

Alex looked over at Chuck. She could tell he was impressed.

"The Russians had their people out after him too," Ebbs said. "It was like war, so our officers ordered a 'no name' policy: we weren't allowed to use our names, just numbers, so if one of us got caught, he wouldn't be able to identify the others.

"We had luck. We found where the Germans had buried their data, and then we found von Braun—or rather he found us and surrendered. He figured he'd be better off in America than with the Russkies. We got him and most of his dope without firing a shot.

"When I bought the boat I was going to call her by my team number, G-13—but then I hit on *No Name*. I liked that better. It's my personal camouflage. So that's *my* story. Now you tell me yours—how you got into radio and rockets and all."

Chuck started telling how their dad had taken him to meet Rosy to learn about radio before he got hurt with his experiments.

"It wasn't *experiments*," Alex interrupted. "Mother'd got a new radio-phonograph for her work with the German music records, and Chuck blew it up trying to find out what made the green tuning light work. He went at it with pliers and a screwdriver until there was a big flash that knocked him down and all the lights went out and Mother screamed and had to take a pill. Dad took the busted Magnavox down to Rosy to get it fixed. Rosy said he'd better teach Chuck about radio before he burned the house down or killed himself—or both!"

Ebbs's mouth was open, half-smiling, as Alex went on gleefully: "Rosy's supposed to be the school's engineer, but he doesn't look anything like an engineer. He doesn't wear a white coat, and he doesn't shave, and he's got this half-smoked cigar in his mouth all the time so his pants and shirts have burn holes."

Chuck shoved at Alex to shut her up.

"Rosy knows radio like he invented it," he said, "and he knows about radar too. He was in the lab in New Jersey when they shot the first radar signal at the Moon. Two and a half seconds later it bounced back—four hundred eighty thousand miles in two and a half seconds!"

He looked at Ebbs.

"Sounds about right."

"He was working on circuit-testing kits some students had sent back," Chuck said. "The starter kits. They didn't work because the students hadn't put them together right. I watched him until he gave me one to fix. Without even looking at the manual I got it right."

Alex piped up. "He didn't look at the book because he mixes things up when he reads." Then she blushed, thinking she'd let her brother down by saying it the way she had.

Ebbs looked at Chuck.

He shrugged and smiled a little. "I guess she told you I left Tech because of my reading. For radio work it doesn't matter so much because if I can watch something being done, I can do it."

Alex butted back in: "Next thing that happened was, Rosy gave him an old Signal Corps field radio to fix with a box of parts and the manual, and with my help reading it we got it going again."

"So when are you going back to school?" Ebbs asked.

"I don't need *school,*" Chuck said. "I've got ideas for inventions I can make on my own. What I need is your help. How about a trade for our helping you with the sailing?"

Ebbs's eyes narrowed.

"See, when I got home from Tech, I went down to the Institute to see if I could make some money helping out. Rosy said I could stick around, but he couldn't pay me. He said the place is going broke with the war over and no more Signal Corps work—but I've got this great idea: make a radar kit the Institute can sell to people like me who want to watch for enemy planes and rockets and space aliens and comets and stuff like that. Alex says you know where they're working with radar, so if you can get me in there so I can study it I'll make up a radar kit for everyday people."

"Hold on!" Ebbs bellowed, straightening up. "Alex got me wrong. I work on space food, not radar."

"But you know the radar people," Chuck insisted. "Alex says you've been to Wallops, and you've met von Braun. I need you to get me to them, get me started."

Ebbs's face was dark.

"Let's go see your Moon Station."

9

THE MOON STATION

"How about I come in and meet your mother first?" Ebbs suggested when they got to the house.

"Right!" said Alex, talking like Ebbs. "I've told her a lot about you. She wants to meet you too."

They could hear music as they walked in. Alex rushed upstairs and knocked on the door to her mother's workroom.

"Mother! Can I bring up Captain Ebbs? She's come to see the Moon Station."

"Oh, lovely!" came a high voice over the music.

The music stopped and her mother opened the door. "Captain Ebbs! Please come in," she said, putting out a jeweled hand. "I'm delighted to meet you! I'm Louise Hart."

Alex's mother wore a dark green dress. The gold chain and pill vial hung around her neck. She smelled of

59

perfume. Ebbs towered over her in jeans and a red shirt. She smelled of sweat.

"Please sit down," Alex's mother said, pointing to a delicate carved chair that looked like it belonged in a museum. "Since Alexis met you, our dinner table has been full of news of your space work. We expect to hear about something going up any day now."

Ebbs loomed over the little chair, nodding and smiling, but she did not sit down.

"Charles's and Alexis's heads are quite filled with space travel," their mother went on, "working at I-don't-know-what up in their Moon Station and making things that burn up and explode. Please, Captain, encourage them to attend to their studies," she said, looking sternly at Chuck, who was hanging back in the doorway.

"Right!" said Ebbs. "They can't get anywhere without the basics."

"I'm so glad to have your support," their mother replied. "Now, Alexis says she's seen a photograph of you with that terrible V-2 rocket."

Mother's test, Alex thought. *She wants to know if I've been making stuff up.*

Ebbs must have guessed as much. She smiled and nodded. "Would you like to see it, Louise? I'll send Alex down with it later. Right now, though, I've come to inspect the Moon Station."

"Oh, splendid! I'm so glad *someone* is going to check it. Their father helped them get started, and he assures me that it's safe, but it looks so precarious, and they spend so much time up there, I'm afraid for them. Do check it, please, and when you get down come back in for tea and give me a full report. They've invited me up, you know—said I could ride in Jeep's device—but I've never been at all good at heights," she said with a slight laugh. "So if you . . ."

"Right!" said Ebbs. "I'll come back in and give a holler if it's not safe, but lemme have a rain check on the tea, OK?"

"Certainly," their mother replied.

"By the way," Ebbs continued, "I've invited them to go sailing with me on the Potomac. You think that would be all right? I've got a sailboat, a twenty-two-footer with all the safety equipment, and they'll be wearing life vests. I'm an experienced sailor," she added, "thirty-five years at it. What do you think?"

"Oh? Well, yes, of course, if they'd like," their mother replied. "When I lived in Germany, I sailed my own boat, the *Little Swan,*" she said, half closing her eyes. "It was much smaller than yours, but we had regattas and I won sometimes. I loved it."

Ebbs was nodding. "When I get 'em trained," she said, "we'll take you out and you'll teach us some tricks."

"Oh, lovely!" their mother said dreamily, turning away. "Lovely."

*　*　*

Alex led Ebbs out to the big tree. "There!" she said, pointing up.

From the ground the Moon Station looked like a bloated squirrel's nest, a silvery roundish lump of what could have been aircraft wreckage snagged in the tree's crown, parts and struts seeming to have wrapped themselves around the major branches on impact. Its ragged, patched-together, bomber-like nose pointed up, its small guidance rockets pointed down, and green and red running lights ran along the sides. Numbered climbing boards nailed into the tree trunk led up to it.

Chuck came with the ladder. There was a gap—the top rung didn't reach the hatch.

"That'll do," Ebbs announced, rubbing her hands together. "I can haul myself up the rest of the way."

She clambered up the ladder, balanced for an instant on the top rung, then pulled the hatch cover.

Too late, Alex remembered the screecher. There was a yowl like a strangled cat.

Ebbs teetered on the ladder top, steadied herself, then looked down.

"Sorry! I forgot to silence it!" Chuck yelled. "It's the theremin. It warns us if there's an alien breaking in. You broke the invisible beam."

Chuck followed Ebbs up the ladder as Alex shinnied up the escape rope.

Jeep sat at the base waving his tail and barking for his ride, not that he really wanted to go up. He hated the swinging, swaying lift in his harness.

Alex's heart sank when she crawled in. Suddenly she saw everything through Ebbs's eyes. In the afternoon light the Moon Station looked clumsy and amateurish with nailed-up gauges; a maze of dials, knobs, wires, and switches; odd pieces of tubing and pipe fitted with faucets and valves marked ROCKET CONTROL #S 1–5; and the greenish cathode ray tube with RADAR written over it looking like a dead eye. The only going things about it were Alex's thriving green mossarium and the Radiometer catching sunlight and spinning like mad.

But Ebbs was delighted. She threw switches, studied the radar tube, pulled levers, cranked the generator, adjusted some rocket-control valves, stomped on the floorboards, shook the pieced-together two-by-fours that supported the shell, pushed at the Plexiglas dome.

"Spaceworthy!" she announced as Alex wound the string around the gyroscope's shaft and pulled hard to get it spinning.

"Good," said Ebbs. "It works like riding a bicycle: once the wheels get spinning you don't tip over. So now we're flying stable. This thing's gonna stay in orbit all right. You guys are good. And I'm glad you've got a Radiometer up here—it works like a solar sail. But tell me how this works," she said, pointing to Alex's magnifying glass mounted over her Girl Scout cooking pot.

Alex could tell something was up. "I'll put water in it," she said cautiously, "aim the glass to catch the sunlight, and boil our food."

"You're going to pour water in space? Where will it go? And then you're going to boil it?" Ebbs asked, her voice rising. "In zero gravity you're going to get water to boil?"

Alex looked blank.

"What happens when mountain climbers try to boil their dinners at high altitudes?" Ebbs asked. "The boiling process requires air pressure. In space, where's the pressure? It's a problem we're working on. How are they going to cook those food tubes I've invented?"

Alex blushed.

Ebbs picked up on her embarrassment. "Hey! That's the fun of exploring: discovering what you don't know and inventing as you go along. What's the point if you already know all the answers? Just add cooking to your to-do list—another problem to solve.

"So now, Chuck," she said, turning to him, "you're the Moon Station's commander, right?"

Chuck nodded.

"Where's your logbook, Commander? You keep a log, right?"

"Lieutenant Alex does that for us," Chuck replied as Alex handed Ebbs the school notebook she'd decorated with a rocket spitting red, yellow, and blue fire. Her mother's old fountain pen was attached to it with a cord tied at the hole she'd punched through the cover.

"What?" Ebbs scoffed. "You use a pen up here? How do you get it to write?"

"Uh-oh," said Alex. "I get it. No gravity, so the ink won't go down?"

"Right," snapped Ebbs, all business. "Only pencils in the Moon Station. Now, I'll come back up here at night to test your navigation with my star bowl. You can adjust it for the seasons. And I'll bring you some algae bags to replace that mossarium. Moss and ferns in a sealed box won't do you any good in space, but you can live on algae—it's nutritious, with protein, minerals, and vitamins. It grows fast and it produces oxygen. Essential for a Moon Station!"

Chuck grimaced as Ebbs went on: "I'm gonna tell VB about this. He's all about getting into space, but you two are already out there. I think he needs to meet some of the people he's building rockets for."

"We need radar, Ebbs," Chuck said.

She gave him a measured look. "Right."

"And it's Alex's birthday," Chuck added.

"Right. I've made a space cake to celebrate. So let's go have some!"

How did she know? Alex wondered.

Smith's Journal

"As I told Alex, I'm kin to Captain John Smith," Ebbs said as she served the space dessert—angel food cake. "What he went through on his trip was probably worse than what you'll go through. Know much about him?" She looked at Chuck.

"No."

"The man who saved Jamestown? You don't know about him?"

"Oh, well, yeah," Chuck said. "A little."

"That's him over there," Ebbs said.

Chuck went over and stared at Smith's grizzled face like he was sizing him up.

Ebbs came and stood beside him. "When he started out all he had in mind was getting away. Any idea what made him want to go?"

Chuck shook his head.

"To make his name," Ebbs said. "To prove himself. When he was a boy they teased and snubbed him because he talked big about what he was going to do. 'I'll show them!' he said to himself. That's what drove him—he was going to make a name for himself, get respect. No matter what it took."

Chuck's eyes were bright.

"Smith was an explorer," Ebbs continued, "going out of bounds, escaping the gravity of the known world in a leaky wooden spacecraft they had to pump and caulk to keep afloat on a voyage of six weeks if they were lucky, three months or never depending on pirates and the weather. Going to the New World in his time was as new and risky as going to the Moon is in ours."

Alex fidgeted. Ebbs noticed. She went over to the card table and handed Alex a wad of marked-up type-written pages.

"Here's what I've taken from his books and journals. I've edited it some, to make up his story for someone like you and Chuck. You've come along just in time—I just finished it. You'll see Smith knew his business, but the knowledge didn't come easy. He worked at learning what he needed to know."

* * *

That night in the Moon Station, Alex started reading aloud.

My parents were dead. I was thirteen and in the way of my guardians' spending what was mine, so they apprenticed me to an old seaport merchant, not a bad man, but there was nothing in that place to hold me. I wanted to go to the places I'd heard men talking about at night when they were drunk and dreaming out loud about Russia, Africa, Constantinople, Virginia—boasting of the rare things they'd seen and found and done, the fortunes they'd won. I wanted adventures of my own, and fortune. I was sick of being an orphaned brat in hand-me-downs.

For a year I had a passing-through schoolmaster not much older than me who taught me to wrestle, cartwheel, juggle, and do magic tricks like whisking a man's handkerchief from his pants pocket and making a penny appear on his shoulder without his knowing.

I wasn't like the others. I never fit in. No home ever felt familiar or comfortable. I heard men talk about home like it was a person, somebody they loved. I didn't know what they were talking about. Anything strange appealed to me more than anything familiar. I realized I was destined to live among strangers when I discovered that foreign tongues came easier to me than to my schoolmates. All my life I've had the knack of picking up strangers' speech almost as quickly as I heard it.

Sure that I was born for something better and bigger than a shop, after my teacher left I sold my school satchel and made up a kit for travel, saving bits of dried beef and biscuit as I waited for my chance. The morning my shop master rushed out distracted to have a rotten tooth pulled, I took what little silver I found in his till, rolled up his heavy blue wool cape, and slipped out the back as if headed to the privy.

I was a week walking and running, heading inland always because I knew they'd look for me along the coast, sleeping in fields rolled up in the stolen cape that went twice around me. I avoided all other travelers, hiding when I saw them, begging milk and bread and morsels of meat and cheese from countrywomen in the late mornings when their men were out in the fields.

The night I got too weak to go on I gave myself up where a faint yellow light drew me. The old woman there took me in and gave me soup and strong tea with cream. She was my angel, asked no questions, took me for what I was. I blessed her in my prayers and left for Portsmouth before dawn the next morning.

When I got there, judging from the hubbub, the next vessel to depart was a boatload of Catholic pilgrims fleeing to Rome, a place I'd heard men at home talk about as older and grander than London even if it was Catholic, so I picked that ship. At the boarding the company was all hurly-burly and confused together, old and young, women and children, topsy-turvy as to who was whose, so it wasn't hard for me to stow away, but I knew stowing away was a dangerous business: stowaways are thought to curse a ship, and me being a Protestant would count as a double curse, so I hid myself well under an overturned lifeboat.

Alex quit reading. The flashlight had grown too dim for her to go on.

"I like him," Chuck said. "I know how he felt about having to get out. Maybe that's why Ebbs gave me his story."

"*Us,*" Alex corrected. "She gave it to *us.* Smith was just a year older than me when he ran away."

"It's not the same for girls," Chuck said.

"Because it's harder," Alex retorted. "Mother's after me all the time about what I *can't* do, mustn't, shouldn't. It's a pain, her going on about growing-up stuff. She says I'm 'unformed,' need shaping, says my character is like a lump of unbaked bread, no way to tell how it will come out unless you shape it, and now she's worked up about Ebbs, thinks she's some sort of religious crank, but Ebbs doesn't talk religious stuff at all. With her it's all about space work."

Chuck peered at Alex, trying to make her out in the darkness. "That what you want to do?"

"Yes," said Alex. "Like Amelia Earhart. How about you?"

"Smith. I want to go out like him."

"Right," Alex said, getting up and reaching for the rope. "I gotta get back to my room in case Mother comes up to tuck me in."

"Remember, we gotta go fix Reggie's car," Chuck said. "I'll come get you later. I jimmied the garage door lock this afternoon. We'll get in tonight OK."

Alex's father was waiting when she came in. "Mrs. King came by while you were up in the Moon Station. Something about her microphone. Somebody saw you going into the assembly room. She put two and two together—she taught Chuck too, you know. She wants an apology and she wants her microphone fixed. Meanwhile, you're on probation.

"You guys!" He sighed, giving Alex a hug.

"She's really mad at me?" Alex asked.

"No, it's not that. You embarrassed her."

Alex felt bad.

Boldly Stated Is Half-Done

The next afternoon coming home from school Alex saw a long black car in the driveway. She grabbed Jeep's collar as she went cold all over, sure it had to do with their fixing Reggie's car the night before. "You hold the funnel. I'll pour," Chuck had whispered. It was so dark Alex couldn't see what she was doing. Later that night she'd had a nightmare: Reggie's father was at the door in his big black hat with legal papers to send them to jail. Now it was for real. The *authorities* had come for them.

A big soldier was knocking at the front door. He wore a pistol on his hip. Another soldier was heading around to the back of the house. The front door opened and the first soldier stepped in as if expected. A minute later he came out and waved. The driver opened the limo's back door. A tall man stepped out. He was well dressed with wavy dark hair combed back like a movie star. The stranger snubbed out his cigarette and went into the house.

The detective, Alex thought. She was scared, thought about running up to Ebbs's, but just then the driver caught sight of her.

"Hi!" he yelled as Jeep barked.

"What's going on?" Alex called in her bravest voice.

"You live here, miss?" the soldier asked. This one wore a gun too.

"Yeah. What's up?" she said, trying to keep the scare out of her voice.

"Your mother's got an important visitor. We're protecting him."

"Who?" Alex asked. "Protecting him from what?"

"Our top rocket man," the soldier replied, "Doctor Wernher von Braun."

Alex was relieved, and astounded.

"The space scientist Doctor von Braun is *here?* Why?"

"Your mother's a translator, right? German songs?"

Alex nodded.

"The doctor is friends with your neighbor, Captain Ebbs, and she knows he likes music—especially German

music, your mother's specialty—so she got the general in charge to arrange a visit while he's up here from Texas, give him a break from his meetings."

"They're inside listening to records?" Alex asked.

"He plays piano, so maybe she's teaching him some songs," the military policeman replied. "VB—he doesn't mind if we call him that—he's really a pretty regular guy once you get over how foreign he is. He's not like what you'd expect one of *them* to be."

"Them?" Alex asked.

"You know, Germans."

"I gotta see him," Alex said, starting toward the door.

"Not yet, miss," the soldier said, stepping in front of her. "We're under orders not to let anyone in. He only

has an hour, so it won't be long. Why don't you get in the back there where he sits and pretend you're a big-deal prisoner like he is."

Alex got in. The car smelled of seat leather and cigarette smoke. A small vase with fresh flowers was mounted beside the door next to a reading light.

"He's a prisoner?" Alex asked.

"It's more like he's a guest of the government—a *protected* guest," the soldier said, putting his hand on his holster.

They talked for a while about spies and Jeep and the soldier's dog back home until the big man came out of the house. Alex scrambled out of the car. As soon as he saw her von Braun smiled and put out his hand.

"So you are Alexis, the youngest one, yes?" he said. "My name is Doctor von Braun."

His chicory-blue eyes bored in like he was reading Alex's mind. She caught her breath. "Yes, sir," she whispered. They shook hands. The rocket man's hand was large and warm.

"Captain Ebbs has told me about you," he said as he studied Alex. "You climb trees like Amelia Earhart to pretend flying, and you do radio with your older brother in the Moon Station, and the two of you watch to catch the weather balloons—is all that correct?"

"Yes, sir," Alex said, feeling her cheeks burn.

"Captain Ebbs says young persons like you are the future of our space program," he continued in his heavy German accent, "so maybe someday we should make something more interesting than little helium weather balloons for you to study, yes?"

"Will we go to the Moon pretty soon?" Alex asked.

The doctor's eyes warmed. "How do you say it, Alexis—'You bet'? Yes. You bet! So now it is very good that I meet you here. You have the key to your Moon Station? I want to see it."

"It—it's not much, sir," Alex stammered. "It's not locked."

"Just so. I want to see it," the doctor said. "Captain

Ebbs told me about it. I know what I'm looking for, and she warned me to be ready for the little electric surprise at the door."

"I'll have to get you the ladder."

"Tell them where it is," von Braun ordered, pointing to his guards. "They will bring it."

"Sir," the soldier in charge protested. "It may not be safe."

"Oh, I'll be careful, officer," von Braun said reassuringly. "It is important that I see what the youth of America are up to, yes?"

Oh, man! I wish Chuck was here, Alex thought. She watched in amazement as the big man in the suit clambered up the ladder. The instant he pulled at the hatch cover the screecher went off again.

"*Ja!*" he roared, jerking back. Then he pitched himself in.

He was inside for what seemed to Alex a long time as she and his guards stood around, eyeing one another and not saying anything, Jeep sniffing each stranger and circling uneasily.

"It is pretty good for what it is," he said when he came down, breathing heavily as he adjusted his tie and dusted off his fine wool suit. "When I was your age we were all for rockets. We did not think too much about making satellites. In that respect you are more advanced than we were, even to planning for food with the algae growing in the nose cone—the influence of Captain Ebbs, yes?"

Alex nodded, too stunned to speak.

"And the theremin—where did you get the idea for that?"

"From a spy story, sir," Alex said. "Chuck built it."

"Yes," the doctor continued thoughtfully, "your older brother. Captain Ebbs has spoken of him too. Well, for what it is, your station is good. The gyroscope you have to stabilize your flight—we learned to use that from your American rocket pioneer, Doctor Goddard. But your navigation equipment? It is ridiculous! That compass you have mounted next to the hand-crank generator— what good will it do you in space? Do you think there is some ultimate North Pole out there? There isn't. You should know that. Discard it!"

"OK. Yes, sir," Alex whispered, her face hot with embarrassment.

"Good," the big man said in his deep voice. "Captain Ebbs says she will give you some lessons with her star bowl. That will help your navigation."

He paused, looking at Alex not unkindly as he thought for a moment. "I do not mean to scold about the compass, Alexis. It is not personal, just a matter of science. You will not be hurt that I point this out, yes? I will send you something to put in its place, a theodolite—the tool surveyors use to measure horizontal and vertical distances. You have seen one?"

What he said made Alex feel better. She stood taller. "Yes, sir, the telescope thing, right?" From her tree perch she'd spied on surveyors using them.

"Yes. I send you one for replacement of that useless compass," the doctor said as he moved toward the car. "So good-bye, Astronaut Alexis," he said with a small bow. "Good cruising in your Moon Station."

As the car started backing out of the driveway he ordered the driver to stop.

"And perhaps when *I* go cruising, you will go with me?" he called.

"Me?" Alex exclaimed, lighting up.

"Tell yourself you're going, and you will," he yelled as the car pulled away. "Boldly stated is half-done—that's my rule!"

Alex waved as hard as she could with both arms high over her head until the car was out of sight. Then she rushed into the house.

"Mother!" she screamed, even though she was under strict orders never to bang in like that on account of her mother's heart. "Mother! Did he tell you about the rockets? His space rockets?"

"No, no, dear," her mother said, coming out of her

room and motioning with her hands that Alex should calm down. "We talked about music. I played some records and we practiced some songs together. With practice he could play well again."

"Yeah, yeah," said Alex impatiently, "but did you know they were guarding the house?" Alex was still bursting with excitement. "The soldier with a gun wouldn't even let me come inside to use the bathroom."

"Oh my," her mother said. "I'm sorry, dear. They told me there'd be security, but he was late. I figured he'd be gone by the time you got home."

"It's OK, Mother," Alex said, talking fast. "Ebbs says he's really important. He'll save us from space rocks, and get us to the Moon and Mars and help us plant colonies like Captain John Smith did because we're running out . . ."

Her mother fluttered her hands and shook her head for Alex to stop going on.

"We didn't get into any of that, dear. With us it was some Mendelssohn they were not allowed to listen to under the Nazis because Mendelssohn was a Jew."

That night, as soon as everyone was seated at dinner, Alex announced, "I met Doctor von Braun! He was here visiting Mother, and there were guards with guns and then he made them bring the ladder so he could go up and look at the Moon Station and the screecher went off, but Ebbs had warned him, and he checked it out, and he says it's good but we need some different navigation equipment he's going to send—"

"What?" John howled, turning red. "Von Braun was here, *in this house?* How could you do it?" he raged at his mother. "How could you help *him?* He's a Nazi war criminal!"

"Oh no, no, dear," their mother replied calmly. "In those days in Germany, everybody who was anybody, especially anyone young who wanted to get ahead, joined the Party. To most people it didn't mean anything; it was just what you did. And Doctor von Braun is an aristocrat, a baron—*Freiherr von Braun*—which means he is royalty, so he is above politics. Alexis says he's a scientist, working on space travel for us."

"Space, *my foot!*" John snarled. "They should hang your fancy *Freiherr!* He used slaves to build Hitler's Vengeance Weapon to bring England to her knees—all so he could get rich, get a big military title and a fancy uniform. He killed thousands—thousands of his slave rocket builders, thousands of helpless civilians! He is evil!"

Alex slumped in her chair like she'd been hit.

"Aw, come off it, John!" Chuck growled. "We're at war with the Russians, or almost, and he's working on stuff we can use against 'em, so what's your problem?

Talk about Vengeance Weapons—what do you call the atom bomb?"

"Boys!" their mother cried, clutching at her chest.

"Enough!" their dad ordered.

"VB didn't . . . !" Alex cried, jumping up from the table. "I'm gonna go ask Ebbs."

"My brother . . . John," Alex gasped when Ebbs opened the door. "He says VB's evil. He says he had slaves and built the rockets to get rich and kill people. Is it true?"

Alex was pale. Jeep stood by her, his tongue lolling.

The big woman pursed her lips. "Come in.

"When I was G-13 we went after him," she said. "It was called Operation Paperclip, which sounds pretty tame, but we were hunting him day and night because he'd headed the German guided-missile project. The Russians were after him too. If we hadn't captured him we would have done everything we could to keep him and his plans from going to anyone else. Capture or destroy was the unwritten order. They even issued *me* a gun," she added as Alex stared at her.

"Then one afternoon this skinny boy comes bicycling down out of the mountains and says he's VB's brother, says VB wants to surrender to us. 'He's up there,' the kid says, pointing. And he was, in a mountain hospital recovering from a crash.

"Right off when I met him all I could think was, if anyone can get us into space it's him."

"So John's wrong?" Alex asked.

"No, he's not wrong about what happened," Ebbs replied. "The Nazis used slaves—used thousands to death—and von Braun knew, just as he built rockets to kill. They were deadly. There's no excusing any of that, just as there's no excusing war itself. I don't mean to let him off, but war is the big evil, Alex. It corrupts everything and everyone. Von Braun let himself get caught up in it for his own purposes.

"What got him off with the authorities was that, late in the war, he'd gotten drunk one night and told the company that the military application of rockets was only part of the picture—a means to getting into space. A Party stooge reported him. The next day the Gestapo arrested him. They searched his room and found his spacecraft drawings and his flight plan to the Moon. They jailed him for diverting military materials to space exploration. When our people heard about his arrest they figured he wasn't really a Nazi—at least they could make the case that he wasn't.

"But here's the big question," Ebbs said, looking steadily at Alex. "Did the end—building a rocket that can get us into space—justify the means, which involved using slaves and murdering civilians? And either way, what do you do with such a person now?"

Alex's jaw trembled. "So should they hang him like John says?"

"No. Even as we were hunting him—when they gave me the gun—all I could think was, *How can I shoot him?* We need him. He's a *maker.* Our survival depends on our making our way into space, Alex—to new worlds, to *making* new worlds. VB's hands and mind are crucial for that. I see him doing good to make up for the bad he did."

That night Alex wrote ASTRONAUT ALEXIS on her door.

12

Icarus

The next afternoon, Chuck told Alex about going to the Flying School. "Nobody was around," he said. "The hangar was empty. I waited for the instructor. When he taxied up in the Piper Cub, I went over and talked to him. He told me the sound in the plane's radio goes in and out. I said I was a student of radio, I'd fix it in exchange for a lesson. I'm going to take my tester and tools over tomorrow. If I fix it he says he'll take me up.

"He let me sit in the cockpit and work the yoke and everything. I could do a takeoff; you aim into the wind to do it. The big thing is, you've got to get the wind going over the wing fast enough to lift off. There's an indicator that shows it. Coming down is easy—you just glide in like those balsa gliders we fool around with sometimes. You want to watch? Want to go over to the airport tomorrow instead of school?"

"Sure," said Alex, thinking about the new name on her door. Flight was flight. Ebbs said VB got started flying small planes.

"Meet me in front of Doc's Variety so they won't know," Chuck said.

Jeep was waiting with Alex when Chuck drove up. "There's an observation deck," he said excitedly. "While I'm fixing the radio you can watch flights taking off and landing. Maybe he'll let you come out and sit in the cockpit with me."

Chuck drove fast, talking about taking off and flying, gesturing as they raced to the airport. When they got there he left Alex and Jeep on the deck and ran over to the flight school's dingy-looking Quonset hut. The Piper Cub was parked nearby.

Chuck yelled something at the hangar door, then went to the plane and climbed in to work on the radio. A little while later he vaulted out, looked around, turned the prop slowly, waved to Alex, then swung himself back in. Alex got a bad feeling in her stomach as Chuck started working the Cub's ailerons and swinging the tail. Suddenly he was out of the cockpit again checking the wheel chocks. He flipped the prop. There was smoke. The engine caught.

"Hey, Chuck! Don't do it!" Alex screamed as he kicked away the chocks and pitched himself back in. The plane started to roll. Alex could hardly breathe.

The flight instructor rushed out yelling and waving his arms as the plane wobbled off, the sun catching it like a golden toy. *Icarus,* Alex thought as the plane straightened out and sped down the runway.

Toward the end of the runway it slowed and lurched to the left, the wing scraping the pavement as Chuck tried to turn the plane around. He was going too fast. The plane skidded, ran through a patch of grass, bounced over a mound of earth, and splashed into the river.

For a long moment there was a silence like sand falling, then pandemonium. Sirens went off. An air horn sounded stunning blasts. Alex raced down the stairs with Jeep close behind and ran as fast as she could to the end of the strip. By the time she got to the wreck emergency vehicles were on their way. They brought Chuck up, muddy and stumbling. Nobody noticed Alex until Chuck saw her and waved.

"I'm OK, Alley!" he yelled, trying to look brave. He pantomimed holding a telephone and mouthed, "Ebbs."

"Who is he? Who are you?" an official demanded.

Suddenly Alex was cool and professional. "I'm his sister," she said. "He's a student of flying. He's learning it like Doctor von Braun. Please help me. I need a telephone."

She ended up in somebody's office. The man got Ebbs on the line. As soon as Alex heard her friend's voice her self-control dissolved. She began to sob so hard she could barely get out the news that Chuck had crashed a plane. "He—yes—he's OK. He had a deal with the flying school pilot. For fixing his radio he was going to get a lesson, but, but he tried to take off himself and it went into the river. I told the people here he was just being like VB."

"I'll be right over," Ebbs said. "Have you called your father?"

"No."

"I will," said Ebbs.

An hour later they were all crowded in the airport security office: Chuck in a corner looking sullen; the officer in charge and some of his people; Alex and Jeep; and the flight instructor, who was sputtering, "He stole it. He stole my airplane and wrecked it." That was when Ebbs walked in.

She looked around, then stared hard at the officer in charge. He recognized her. He mouthed the word "paperclip."

She nodded.

Alex noticed and glanced at Chuck. He had noticed too.

"I'm representing the boy's parents," she said.

"This is a serious matter," the officer began. "He maybe thinks it was a prank, but it's really what the owner says—theft—not to mention violation of all sorts of federal flight regulations."

Ebbs spoke up in her army voice. "Perhaps there was a misunderstanding." She turned to the flight instructor. "My young friend here was doing a radio repair on your aircraft when it happened, right? He was in the plane with your permission, correct? In exchange for his work he was to get a lesson—yes?"

The man tried to speak, his lips working like a goldfish, but Ebbs kept talking and turned back to the officer in charge.

"It could be attempted theft," she continued in a respectful tone, "but it *could* be he was trying to give himself the lesson he'd earned: taxi down a little, brake, turn, and taxi back. But he got going too fast, couldn't stop and turn, so he ran it into the river. Looked at that way, it's reckless and careless—but not criminal."

The officer shook his head. "It's a whole lot more than reckless and careless, Cap . . . ah, ma'am—an unlicensed person running an aircraft out on an active runway without tower clearance or anything—and what do you do about this man's aircraft?"

"We'll take care of the repairs," Ebbs replied evenly. "They've already pulled it out. I checked it before I came in. There's damage to the wing and some struts and the wheel assembly, but nothing that can't be fixed. We'll cover it."

The airport security people talked things over. "We could charge you with criminal trespass," the chief announced, glaring at Chuck, "but we're not going to. We'll give you the benefit of the doubt under the, ah, *circumstances*," he said, glancing at Ebbs, "provided you satisfy the owner that you will pay for everything."

"Done," said Ebbs, nodding to the instructor, who was already holding her check. "Right?"

When it was over and they were standing outside, Ebbs turned to Chuck, her eyes narrowed, her voice low.

"Mister, if you were in the army under my command, starting now you'd be in jail doing real hard duty."

Riding home, Chuck was blithe. "You know what, Alley? I really was trying to take off. I just wasn't going fast enough. The airspeed indicator was still showing red when I got to the end of the runway. I tried to work the Cub's brakes as I turned, but things were happening so fast I couldn't. I wasn't afraid, though. I had this great taste in my mouth—like when I swing on that fraying grapevine over the ravine and I'm hanging at the end of the pitch and I don't know whether I'm going to snap and crash or make it back—and either way's OK."

13

THE SHOPLIFTER

A few days after the plane crash Chuck showed Alex a sketch he'd made. "A catamaran," he explained, "a boat that floats on pontoons. I got the idea at the toy store." He lurched around in the Moon Station to show how the boat would go. "They just got in a model airplane engine smaller than my palm. It weighs less than an egg. All of a sudden I saw it powering a radio-controlled boat.

"I've figured out all the radio stuff. We'll move the rudder with electromagnets activated by a radio signal. No gears or anything.

"So here's where you come in, Alley: you're going to wind the magnets. You're gonna take a medium-sized nail and wind it with a length of insulated wire to make a coil. When you run a current through it a magnetic field will set up and move the rudder. You with me?" Chuck asked, pointing to the drawing. Alex wasn't. She didn't understand how winding wire around a nail could move anything.

"I figure we can make up a really neat package," Chuck said, "something the Institute can sell by mail with the boat pieces precut, the engine and fuel tank just as they come from the store, navy decals and flags, and one of Rosy's kits with the transmitter and receiver parts for the radio control. And your electromagnets."

Alex hadn't yet wound a magnet that worked when she told Ebbs how Chuck had figured to guide the boat with them. Ebbs was impressed. "It's like one of VB's solutions," she remarked. "Simple. He'd like that."

A week later Chuck showed up in Alex's room with the motor. It was finned and shiny with a tiny porcelain glow plug screwed in at the top, CHAMPION written on it in minuscule red letters.

Alex was still struggling with the electromagnets when Chuck said they should do a water trial. They went down to the creek. Chuck fixed the engine to the catamaran's bridge, locked the rudder so the boat would go in wide circles, and got the engine going. It snarled like a buzz saw as it sent the boat zooming around until the fuel ran out. The exhaust stank.

"We need more range," Chuck muttered. "Another tank."

Alex had about given up winding magnets. She figured getting the tank was the one thing she could do to help. She knew where to find it. She and Jeep walked up to town. She slipped into the toy store without being noticed. The model airplane parts were kept behind the side counter. She bent down, trying to hide behind it as she reached for the tank.

"Hey, kid! Get out of there!" the clerk yelled. "Whatcha got in your hand?"

As the man approached, Jeep's ruff went up. He began to bark. The dog looked huge.

The clerk picked up a stool and held it out to fend him off.

Alex wanted to throw down the tank and run, but she couldn't. She was frozen.

The clerk's face was fleshy and splotched with fury. There was a dark hairy bump in the center of his chin that bobbled when he spoke. Alex stared at the bump. The tank felt like it was burning in her hand.

The manager was standing behind the clerk now.

"What's your name?" the manager demanded.

Alex felt like she'd been hit in the stomach. She couldn't get breath to yell "Sic!"

"What's your name?"

"Alex," she gasped.

"Alex what?"

"Ebbs," she panted.

"What's your phone number?"

"I don't know."

The man looked up "Ebbs." There was only one. A new listing. He called the number.

"We've got your daughter here. Caught her stealing. Yeah, Alex. Her dog's here too. We've been losing all kinds of stuff—engines, props, parts. OK, we'll hold her.

"You in a gang?" he demanded while they waited for Ebbs.

"No."

Ebbs looked grim but she didn't let on anything when she came in. Alex couldn't hear much of what she said to the manager as she paid for the tank, but she saw her shake her head when the word "gang" came up.

"If I ever see you in here again I'm calling the police," the manager yelled as Ebbs led Alex out. Jeep jumped into the back of Ebbs's old coupe and sank down small.

"Did you do this for a thrill or to help Chuck?" Ebbs asked as they drove off.

Alex didn't answer. She felt too sick with shame to speak.

"I think I know," Ebbs said.

14

SAVING CHUCK

"I'm gonna get you two straightened out right now or know the reason why," Ebbs said. "First stop, the junkyard where you traded the spoons. The one on Seventh Avenue, right?"

"Yes," Alex answered. "But why are we going there? We never stole from *him*."

"Right. With him it was the other way around."

As they parked Alex pointed to the hairy keg of a man in grease-stained coveralls sprawled on a sofa in front of the office.

"That's Hector."

Hector recognized Alex, but there was something about Ebbs that made him squint through pig eyes as she strode up, hands on her hips.

"You know this girl, right?" Ebbs demanded in her army voice.

"Yessum," the junk man said, slowly getting up.

"Comes here with her brother, right?"

"Yessum."

"Came here a while ago with some silver spoons, right?"

"Dunno about that," Hector mumbled vaguely. "Lots of stuff comes through . . ."

"Stolen property," Ebbs snapped. "I want 'em back or we're going to the police." She pulled out a five-dollar bill. "This will make you whole for that extinguisher."

They left with the spoons.

"Now we're gonna go see Chuck."

Alex put a finger to her lips as they entered the house and headed up the stairs. "I'm coming up with Ebbs," she called softly when they got to the attic door.

"Our invention," Chuck said, smiling proudly as he pointed to the model.

"Yeah," said Ebbs as she opened her purse and pulled out the tank. "And here's one of the parts. You send her out for it?"

Chuck shot Alex a surprised look. "No."

"Well, she got caught trying to steal it for you—for that," Ebbs said, pointing to the catamaran. "The motor must have cost a lot. You send her out for that?"

Chuck's eyes narrowed.

"Did you?" Ebbs repeated.

"No," Chuck muttered. "I got it myself."

"Right. You stole it."

Chuck didn't say anything.

Ebbs picked up the catamaran and began turning it roughly in her big hands as if she might crush it. "You told me about the Institute needing new kits, so you've come up with one—but to do it you've been stealing from toy stores like some sort of Robin Hood."

Chuck stood silent.

"Not that you're all that noble," Ebbs said as she laid out the spoons.

They were standing in a tight circle, Ebbs towering over them as she stared at Chuck, waiting for him to say something.

Chuck looked at her, unblinking, his head level.

Jeep was panting, his tail between his legs as he looked from face to face.

Chuck began speaking in a hollow voice. "Mother thinks I'm going to do big things. . . . At school they laugh at me."

"So you steal to get even?"

Chuck's face tightened. "Forget it, Ebbs. I'm a dud. That's why they threw me out of Tech. I can't do that stuff. It makes me crazy. The others think I'm dumb, and

I guess I am, but I'm getting even. They can read and do math better than me, but I'm getting away with more than they ever dreamed of. And in the end when I get caught for something *big* I'll jump off a bridge or take a fistful of pills or hang myself—I've thought it all out: I'll do myself in."

Alex began to sob.

Suddenly Ebbs was Captain Ebbs again, eyes glittering, chin set. "That sort of talk makes me furious," she said. "What about everybody who has to clean up after you—the people who love you—your mother, your father, Alex? You kill yourself, their hurt lasts forever. You think talk like that's brave? It's cowardly, and I don't think you're a coward. Not being able to read fast and compute isn't what got you thrown out. They sent you home for taking stuff—'getting even,' as you put it. And what's that about? The students you stole from, the toy store owner—what did they ever do to you? And what about the other people like Alex you mess up in your wake? Worst of all, you're stealing from yourself, poisoning your self-respect."

Chuck's eyes went dull. "How did you find out?"

"I wasn't a CIC agent for nothing, Chuck. I did a little investigating, called the dean at Tech. I checked you guys out—that's how I knew about Alex's birthday."

Ebbs looked down at the model she was holding. She

paused, seemed surprised to find it in her hands. "This thing," she said slowly, "the person who dreamed this up is no dud. We need folks who can think things through to their hands. You've got a gift, Chuck. I know it, Alex knows, Rosy knows, and this boat you've built proves it. Plus, you care about some really important things. Most folks don't, so they just slog along bored and not very useful. But you've got something precious," she added in a gentler voice. "So please don't go around risking it."

Chuck slumped and shook his head.

Ebbs put down the model, stepped close to Chuck, and put her big hands on his shoulders. "A while ago you asked me to get you to some people who are working with radar. Play by my rules," she said, gripping him hard and rocking him slowly back and forth as she spoke. "Play by my rules and I will."

Chuck shook himself free. "How?" he asked, his mouth twisted. "You said you didn't work with radar."

"Something will come up. So starting now you've got to play by my rules—both of you."

"What rules?" Chuck asked, his voice half-strangled.

"Simple! No more tricks like climbing the radio tower, borrowing airplanes, stealing toy motors, or fiddling with people's cars. Get a police record—which that car caper would have gotten you for sure had Mr. Comstock not noticed some gooey stuff by the gas flap—

get a record and I'll never be able to get you the security clearance you'll need for what I have in mind."

"What would I ever need a security clearance for?"

"You know as well as I do. For me to get you anywhere near Wallops, you'll need a security clearance."

"Why?" Chuck asked. "Why are you bothering?"

"Because I think you've got some special fire, and because when I make a friend I hang on to him. Maybe you didn't choose me, but I've chosen you, and I'm not going to let you go ruin yourself if I can help it."

She stared at Chuck for a long moment. "So those are my rules."

She turned to Alex. "As for you, starting now you're going to say no when he starts going wrong. And absolutely no more stealing!"

Alex backed away, shaking her head. "No more stealing—OK. But I can't stop him from anything. Not even Dad can."

"Can you say no to him?" Ebbs asked. "Can you say no to yourself? To try and save his chance and to save yourself, can you say *no* and at least *try* to stop him?"

"I guess," Alex whispered.

Chuck lifted his head slowly to stare at his sister, wide-eyed, expressionless, like someone in a fever.

"Right!" said Ebbs. "We're on a new page here."

15

STOWAWAY

That night in the Moon Station, Alex didn't feel like talking. She felt bad, the cause of everything coming to a head. Chuck was grim-faced.

"All this Ebbs stuff is like Mother saying I've got genius in my hands," he muttered. "They don't know. They don't know who I am. I'm different, I'm dark, I don't look like anyone in the family, I'm left-handed—I'm not like the rest of you. When my hand got big enough— I was seven or eight—Mother gave me this ring," he said, taking it off and showing it to Alex. Alex knew it. It was a gold ring with a deep-set sapphire.

"Look what's written on the inside," he said. "It's Carlus, my name in Latin. She told me it was a gift from someone when she was in Europe. It's really old." It looked old. The stone was worn, its bevels dulled. "That's all she knows about me. My first name."

He grew silent.

They sat there for a moment. Finally, Alex picked up Ebbs's manuscript. Without asking, she began reading aloud again from Smith's journal.

The first day out, cramped and hungry in my hiding, I fed myself on what I imagined I'd see and do in Rome, but then the ship began to pitch so hard and the sailing got so rough it drove me out from my hiding.

When they discovered me a stowaway, and worst of all a Protestant, they threw me overboard, the sailors swearing God would drown them all if I stayed on board. Not a voice was raised to save me as they told their rosaries loud to be spared my screams as they pitched me in like another Jonah.

When I hit the water I counted myself dead, but then my luck, which always comes to me in threes, came on in the form of a pirate ship that had been tracking my pilgrims just over the horizon. They picked me up as a slave to sell. When I told them what sort of ship their quarry was, they let it go, not out of mercy but because pilgrim luggage wasn't worth their trouble.

I was with them all that summer learning their pirate tricks of surprise, our faces made up fierce and reckless like actors, screaming and roaring as we boarded to drown our own terror.

My tutor was a jagged three-inch piece of mirror glass I could use as a weapon if need be. I studied in it for hours to cast fire from my eyes so you'd know that once you took me on, if you didn't kill me I was going to do my best to kill you. I was small but quick, and I could wrestle better than anybody. The scars I earned in that trade soon made me look older than my years.

The night we landed at Marseille I dropped off the side naked as a fish, my boots and clothes in a tarred bag at my side. I swam to shore with a gold coin in my cheek and a sailor's knife in my teeth.

I hung around the port, watchful lest my old shipmates see me and try to get me back, juggling and cartwheeling in the dark and poorer places to pick up food and news until I snared what I needed: stale bread and word that the King of Hungary had work for soldiers. I set out to the northeast. Having now my scars and pirate knowledge, I hired on to fight the Turks attacking Vienna.

I was some years in that business, learning the work of a journeyman soldier and teaching my

fellows the tricks of fireworks for signaling and terrorizing until, to show off my bravery to my employer, I volunteered for single combat against the Turks' champion.

We fought in an open field in sight of both armies. I killed my man with a lucky stab to the eye, but then the Turks put forward a second champion saying I hadn't fought fair, as if any Turk ever does. No choice and no matter, I dispatched the second one as well by cartwheeling around him to chop at his heel strings. As he fell my slash sent his neck gushing blood like a bilge pump. Then the Turks called forth their third champion. This one was timider, a slow, cautious dancer as he sought to avoid me. I tripped him with a wrestling trick—a quick side step—and took his head too for my pile. They had many more champions, I'm sure, but no more volunteers.

For this service the Hungarian king awarded me the title Captain and a coat of arms featuring my three Turks' heads. Now I, a poor man's son, was a Captain in the Austrian Imperial Guard with a coat of arms and a chamois leather bag of gold as well.

I counted that adventure my third piece of luck, but that bag of gold and all that's passed through my hands since I've never liked as much as some men do because I seem to smell the stench of dead flesh on every piece. Gold remembers; it is the one metal that never tarnishes.

There I was, by reputation the terror of Turks who swarmed before us, but then my luck turned as it always has for me: three bads following three goods. In what was meant to be a minor skirmish I went down with a gash deep in my leg. That night I lay faint and cold, bleeding to death when the pickers found me—the folks who come out after battles to strip the dead for clothing and treasure. By what I wore they recognized I was no common soldier, so they staunched my wound and cleaned me up for ransom, but unfortunate for them and me they stripped and shaved me so bare that no one believed I had any significance at all, so I ended up bald as an egg, sold as a common slave in the Constantinople market.

Constantinople, that magic-sounding place I'd dreamed of in my dull merchant's shop back in England: it was now all mine to see, but it didn't look so fine through a prisoner's eyes.

The pasha who bought me riveted a heavy iron ring around my neck with an outsticking spike shaped like a sickle to grab me by and haul me about. He used me badly. I was the lowest of the low, but I kept up my spirits by thinking of nothing but learning the Turk language.

One afternoon my pasha came alone to where I

was working by myself threshing grain. He spat on me for being a Christian. In a black rage I hurled my threshing bat into his gut. He went down doubled. My next blow did for his head.

I stripped him, put on his Turk clothes and knapsack, buried his body in straw and was off on his horse with the heavy spiked iron still around my neck.

As I rode off I remembered other times I'd escaped in another man's clothes and wondered if someday someone would slip into mine to make his escape smelling my stink of fear and feeling the last of my own damp warmth.

I rode for my life. Wherever one road crossed another there were arrows with pictures: to Persia, a black man with white spots; to China, a sun; to Russia, a cross.

For sixteen days I rode for Russia, afraid of being identified as a runaway by that iron around my neck with its spike sticking out, my shaved head and my ignorance of the land and language. For food I played the beggar, juggling, cartwheeling, and grinning like an idiot until I reached the Russian garrison on the River Don, where my newly grown red hair and freckled skin caught the eye of a Russian lady. She had my iron removed.

For a time the lady Calamata befriended me. When she finally turned me out it was with a piece of news and a jewel to remember her by, a diamond. Before she told me her news she taught me how to test if a diamond be true: a true one pressed against ice will melt it. Glass will not, nor will any other jewel.

Her news was of a means to get back to England: a group of English merchants had come to the czar at Moscow seeking permission to trade English woolens for sables and timber. Sure that I knew the Russian tongue better than anyone else in that group and certain that the czar was after warmer stuff than cloaks and blankets, she sent me to Moscow to make myself useful. I went in the guise of a priest. The high-collared shirt hid the scar of the iron ring I'd worn.

Her hunch paid off. It was how to make guns and gunpowder the czar was after, and I knew that business from my pirate time. So you see now how my hands are still stained black from kneading sulfur, saltpeter, and charcoal with old urine to make fire signals, smoke bombs, lightning, and blasts to blow down walls and forts.

In disguise I finally made it back to England. I was twenty-five when I got home, scarred for life from that ring—a body mark that was to fascinate my Native American captors, as did my black-veined hands. To my former neighbors' surprise I now had a title, a coat of arms, a sable collar to hide my mark, and some gold, not that they sneered at me any the less. New titles and new gold did not count as much with them as old.

Alex put down the manuscript and looked over at Chuck. "Smith was starting out new like you."

"You think I'm like him—like that?"

"Yes."

Alex slid down the rope and headed across the lawn toward the house with Jeep at her side. She stopped when she heard a low, whistling owl call. Her father said a single owl called when someone died, but if another owl answered it meant good news for anyone who heard. Alex held her breath. There was an answering call. She sighed with relief.

16

THE NO NAME

The next morning Alex helped her father weed. Working with dirt and plants made her feel better. She told her dad about getting caught stealing. He already knew. "Hold to your pledge, Alex," he said. "Stealing leads to a world of trouble."

That afternoon Ebbs said the weekend weather looked promising, so they should go sailing on Saturday. "Old clothes," she ordered, "the oldest you've got, and your most beat-up sneakers. If your dad's got any old white shirts he can spare and some old hats, bring those along too. And dog food. I've got everything else."

On Saturday morning Alex, Chuck, and Jeep rode with Ebbs down to the river to see the *No Name*. Ebbs fumbled and bumped into things on shore, but on board her moves were exact. She handed out heavy kapok life vests that made them all look like red blocks. For Jeep she'd rigged a harness belowdecks, a sort of hammock that held him dangling like a carcass, his paws barely touching the bilge boards. He grumped and grunted as she fitted him into it. It offended his dignity to ride that way, but Ebbs was firm. She was firm about everything. Jeep could have escaped. Ebbs left it loose enough for him to get out if they capsized, but he felt it his duty to stick with them.

"Shipshape is more than housekeeping," Ebbs explained as she showed them how everything had its special place. "It's survival. We're on our own out there, nobody can help us; we might as well be a mile down in a cave. Something goes wrong, it's on us to fix it—replace a broken halyard, stitch up a torn sail, jury-rig a snapped mast. We've got to be ready for anything, so you've gotta learn the four basic sailors' knots: reef, square, bowline, and half hitch. They're not easy. It took me a lot of practice to get them right, but like my father said, 'Patience is never wasted.' If I can manage 'em with my clumsy fingers, you can too."

Ebbs pushed them off from the dock and ordered Chuck to raise the mainsail. A slight breeze swelled it and they were off. Alex was surprised how just that wisp of wind could make the heavy boat heel as it glided them along.

Ebbs showed Alex how to set the anchors and check the tide chart. "And pump," she added, reaching down for a black tube the length of her arm with a handle on top. "You'll stick the bottom end into the bilge and pump it as dry as you can. In weather and rough water we'll take turns."

The current and the outgoing tide carried the *No Name* along, but they were going faster than the water, as Ebbs proved by tossing out a chip that they shot past. The river had a strong smell, something between old salad and wet dog.

"Smith mapped all this," Ebbs said, one hand on the tiller, the other pointing to the shore. "The chart he made shows that point over there. He knew it would prove useful. It's where barrels of tobacco the later colonists called Virginia gold got loaded on ships to London. Helps you understand the connectedness of water, how it links up everywhere. Stick your hand into the Potomac here and you're connecting with London docks, or whatever port you name."

Suddenly the river wasn't empty. A cruise ship came toward them heading up to Washington. Ebbs shifted the mainsail, tacking and working the tiller to steer them away. They waved, the ship's captain tooted, and soon they were dancing in its wake, Jeep swinging like a clock pendulum in his harness. He gave Alex a baleful look as

she laughed and rocked. Chuck stayed forward, leaning against the mast, silent.

"Mount Vernon," Ebbs announced as they glided soundlessly past a long green sloping meadow that led up to a large white mansion with columns. "George Washington's plantation. There's his tobacco pier. Story goes, he once tried to skip a silver dollar across the river from that pier."

Alex scrunched up her face to judge the distance. She shook her head. "Bet it wasn't his dollar."

"Check the tell tail," Ebbs ordered.

"The what?" Alex asked.

"The wind indicator. That strand of horsehair tied to the mainstay."

Alex looked. The tell tail had begun to droop. Gradually the wind stilled to nothing.

Ebbs turned to Alex. "Looks like we'll be drifting for a while, so tell me, do you know what *Quo vadis* means?"

Alex shook her head. It sounded like something John would ask.

"It's Latin for 'Where are you going?'" Ebbs explained. "Tell me where you're going."

"Doctor von Braun told me I'm going to fly in space someday. He said maybe I'd go with him."

"Great!" Ebbs exclaimed. "But how are you going to get ready? What are you going to study? What's your work going to be? The test pilots I work with—the people who are going to be our astronauts—they didn't train to be passengers. They're medical doctors, physicists, chemists, biologists. You've told me where you're going—now I want to know what you're going to do to get yourself there. Chuck's talking about doing electronics, but right now he's luffing, which is a sailing term meaning his sails are flapping idle so he's not going anywhere. I'll get to him. What I want to know from you is, how are you going to get to liftoff? What are you interested in?"

"Rockets, space, radio . . ."

"Right," said Ebbs. "So what are you going to do with your life?"

Alex squirmed. It felt like she should have nailed that down by now.

When the wind picked up again they came about and started back upriver. Suddenly Ebbs winched up the keel, handed Alex the tiller, and pointed to a pier. "Get us there," she ordered.

Alex swung the tiller, but the boat didn't respond. She tried fishtailing it. Nothing happened. The *No Name* turned like a leaf in the current and started drifting downstream at a pretty good clip.

"It's like you," Ebbs said. "Drifting with no plan. Having no life plan is like having no keel, no control over where you're going. You don't have to hold to it, but it's high time you both start mapping out where you're going in life, what you *might* do. You can always change course later on, but it's good to have a starting point— something to measure your progress against. So here's a project to start you both off," she announced as she let the keel down and brought the boat about again.

"I need deckhands for a cruise—one-way down the Potomac and out into the Chesapeake to Tangier Island, where I've got a friend who will put us up. It's my vacation. I want to spend it on the *No Name,* but I can't do it without crew. If you two say OK, and your parents agree after they come and check things out—your mother especially, since she's the sailor—your pay will be a dollar a day each. I'll get you back home before school starts. As we go, we'll make like we're Captain Smith's crew, mapping the shoreline as we follow the chart he made and searching like he did for the lost Roanoke colonists I'll tell you about. We'll carry all our food. I've got some great new recipes going."

Chuck caught Alex's eye and raised his eyebrows.

"I saw that," Ebbs said with a laugh as she got out the navigation chart. "As we go along we'll tuck in here and there for ice-cream cones, bread, and suchlike, but you guys will be my food testers. I've been living on my new stuff for months now, and I'm not wasting away, am I?"

Ebbs rolled out a much-thumbed sea chart and pointed to the upper left corner. "Here's where we are, Washington," she said. As the heavy paper curled tightly over her left hand she pointed down to its far right. "And here's where we're going. You're going to mark our progress, Alex, so hold the chart," she said as she reached for a pair of dividers that looked like heavy tweezers with sharp points at the ends. "You'll use these to work out our distances," Ebbs explained. "You spread them against the miles scale to set the distance, then swing them point to point down our course. We'll follow Smith's course from here at Washington downriver to the bay. As a crow flies it's about a hundred and thirty miles to our jump-off at Smith Point.

"From there out to Tangier it's about twenty miles straight across open water, but of course we'll be zigging and zagging to keep the wind, so it's going to be up to you, Alex, to keep us on course following the buoys against the map and working the compass."

On the map Tangier looked tiny and far away, barely a gray-brown dot against the bay's blue green. "It's the top of an undersea hill," Ebbs explained. "That's all any island is, a mountaintop sticking up out of the water.

"From Washington down to Smith Point it'll take us five to ten days, depending on the wind and tides. Then to the island, a day—with any luck. If we don't make it in one we'll anchor and sleep on board. It'll be a little tight, but we'll manage. You can sleep down below—there's room, but it gets stuffy—or I'll wrap you in tarps and tie you down on deck so you won't roll off in your sleep."

Alex didn't like the idea of getting tied down. She and Jeep moved around at night, but sleeping in the space under the deck didn't sound like much of an alternative.

"What's the island like?" she asked.

"Flat. One church. Three miles long, a mile across. It's close enough to Wallops that you can hear the roar when they do a test firing. If they launch we'll get to see the flare."

"Great!" Chuck exclaimed. "Any chance they'll do one when we're there?"

"Launch times are classified," Ebbs said, "but I hear from my friend Pete they're getting ready."

17

UNDER WAY

Alex had hardly slept watching for clouds and shooting stars and packing and repacking her knapsack. The only nonessential things in it were the last pages of Smith's journal and her space rock. Chuck's pack, though, was bulging with binoculars, tools, and spare radio parts, and then there was the Signal Corps radio itself. Ebbs objected to his bringing it. It was heavy and would take up a lot of space in the small cockpit, she said, but he wouldn't go without it. "To be sailing just across from Wallops, where they're doing all that rocket and radar work and *not* listen in? No, ma'am. I might pick up something really important."

"Like what?" Alex asked.

"Like when they're going to launch."

They set off in fair weather on an easy breeze that

sent the *No Name* skimming past farms fragrant with mowing and new-turned earth.

They rode along for a while, absorbing the quiet music of the boat cleaving water. "I didn't want to tell you before," Ebbs said, "but one reason I wanted you two along is so I wouldn't run into ghosts and have to scare them off by myself. When a sailor named Joshua Slocum went sailing alone around the world a hundred years ago he met ghosts and had to talk all the time to get them to go away. He talked to himself until he ran out of things to say, then started singing. He sang himself hoarse. He got really scared when his voice gave out. I wanted you two along so I wouldn't have to do all the talking to keep off the ghosts. Not that I *believe* in ghosts, but Slocum didn't either. When you're alone too much weird things happen. It's in his book."

Ebbs spotted a good mooring place. Alex set the anchors. After supper they sat silent, looking into the fire. Then Ebbs began to study the sky. Stars shone like dots and bands of Queen Anne's lace in a deep slate field.

Suddenly something bright streaked overhead.

"A rocket!" Chuck exclaimed.

"Nope," said Ebbs. "An opener for the Perseid meteor shower we get here late summer every year— just as Smith predicted. That was one of his powers that Powhatan pretended to find marvelous—Smith could make fires appear in the sky. But of course Powhatan knew to expect them."

There were some last soft robin calls. The night air had taken on a sweet, damp pine fragrance. Sometimes a breeze drifted in off the river, a zephyr so different from the land breeze that Alex wondered how two such different bands of air could lie so close together. Now and then there were night bird calls, surprising but not startling. Even the *plop* of a large fish did not startle Alex now. From the other side of the river came the idle barking of a bored dog.

"You bring any Smith pages along?" Ebbs asked.

"Yup," said Alex, unwrapping them from the wax paper at the bottom of her pack. She began reading aloud.

I could have gone on from adventure to adventure, a freebooting soldier-for-hire until I died forgotten in some unknown place, but I knew I was capable of better. But better what? I asked myself. Doing what? My gold afforded me a year living alone in a rough country hut, toughening my body and training myself for anything, reading Machiavelli on war and Marcus Aurelius and some other Romans again to learn what made for a good leader. I learned that what counts most is being absolute master of oneself, resolute, never wavering, never undecided, never without a Next. I read Caesar's Gallic Wars *and decided I'd be a writer too.*

Shares in Virginia being offered for sale, I bought one and began to study Mr. Hariot's book about Roanoke. His was the only text there was about life in Virginia, and it had pictures. I read it over and over and taught myself the few Algonquin words he gave. A week before my twenty-sixth birthday I sailed for America.

My companions—we were 105 in all—were all for finding gold. Talking with them I discovered they knew nothing about settling, building, farming, or defending themselves in a raw and hostile land. They said they'd pay somebody else to make their fortress and feed them—but what if there was no food to buy and no one to do that work? What use would their money be then? I knew a little about Virginia from Mr. Hariot's book. They knew nothing.

Most of my fellows called themselves gentlemen. Despite my experience and captaincy they classed me with the few, twelve only, described as laborers.

I saw trouble coming in the leaders' ignorance. I made so much trouble demanding plans and training that before we landed Captain Wingate had me locked in the brig as a traitor to be hung. My dog stayed close. But for his company I'd have gone mad. We spoke to each other. My jailors heard us talking together and thought me crazed.

I arrived at Virginia in the brig, my dainty gentlemen with their manicured hands intending to hang me, but then they opened the orders box we'd been sent out with and discovered I was supposed to be one of their Council. Me! A commoner of no breeding ranked with them!

They wouldn't have it, never mind orders. They voted to keep me under guard while they set the lesser sorts to building the fort—but what did these goldsmiths, tailors, and perfumers know about fortress making? They built a bird's nest of twigs and mud while our gentlemen scratched for gold, dug for gold, dreamed of gold, and lived off the ships' stores.

Our commoners were as gold-smitten as the others, lazy except for mining and panning, and anyway they knew nothing about planting. For the moment grains of gold counted for more with them than grains of wheat. It was the fable out of Aesop: they were all singing crickets, but the song those crickets made was the dreary rattle of barren silt in their sluice pans.

For a few weeks the Natives were glad enough to trade their corn for our copper goods and edge tools, but our President managed this business badly, paying too much for too little and so spoiling the market to the point our grocers grew insolent and demanded guns for grain.

When things became dire enough I was released and sent out to get food because I knew something of the Natives' tongue. I went several days upriver to where our needs and profligacy were not so well known. When my offers to trade glass beads for corn did not prevail I let fly with my muskets, going for broke as was my manner always, we few collectors greatly outnumbered in everything excepting my leader courage. My men said I seemed in myself the glaring force of a thousand.

I got us a boatload of corn, but on returning I found our fort attacked, seventeen hurt, a boy slain, and only a cannon blast from one of our ships sending the Natives off.

Finally seeing me as the one who best knew the business of providing and defending, the people turned to me for fort building and defense. Right away I set them to training at arms, baking bricks, grinding shells to make mortar—at least such as could. So many were ill! Within days of my taking command scarce ten could stand, such extreme weakness and sickness oppressed us.

Then treachery: while I was off on another food-gathering trip, our gentlemen commandeered the one remaining seagoing vessel. They were about to turn tail and run themselves back to England with the last of our supplies when I surprised them.

They were more and better armed, but they knew I meant it when I yelled, 'Stay or sink.' Wingate's face I well remember, ferret-eyed when he saw me, his mouth curling ugly, and he was never a pretty man. He knew I'd kill him if I had excuse even if it meant my own death, and now was opportunity. I made my face show my joyful determination. They came cringing back to be kept by the heels and sent as prisoners to England, and so it fell to me to lead all.

From that day on my rule was no work, no food—gentleman and commoner alike. No more gold hunting, not that there was ever much found there. Now we panned for food in plain dirt, dug it, grubbed it, hoed it—every man a farmer and none excused.

Spirits improved. Nothing cures despair like work. Giving them purpose, I gave them hope. Without hope there can be no endeavor. That much

I got from my Romans, that and what some took for ruthlessness. In easy times some kindness will do, but hard times demand iron rule, and our times were hard indeed. We were starving.

I went on another mission after food. The Natives surprised the party I'd left behind with the small boat and killed two. Alone and twenty miles inland I was beset by two hundred. Two of them I slew, but I got shot deep in the thigh and had many other arrows stuck in. At last, trapped in a swamp, they took me prisoner and tied me to a tree.

I knew enough of their language to demand that I, a chief, be brought to theirs. I would not treat with any lesser man, though they might kill me if they would. When their Chief came to me I signaled I had a great matter to discuss with him but would not do so bound.

Untied, I showed him what I had in my pocket wrapped in an oiled cloth: a round ivory compass. I demonstrated the roundness of the Earth and how the sun chased night round about the world continually. He took this for great magic and led me to the center of Powhatan's village through a file of armed men, their torsos and faces streaked red and black. They all made grim to terrify me, but they

*couldn't: I put my Turks' heads in my mind and
began a roaring chant to unsettle them.*

*When I came before Powhatan it was cold. I
was still wearing what they'd pulled me from the
swamp in. He was sitting before a fire, upon a seat
like a bed covered with a great robe made of deer
and raccoon skins and decorated with rare shells
he'd traded for.*

*Powhatan was holding the ivory globe com-
pass. I gave him to understand I could show him
stranger things still—that I could even make fires
in the sky, for it had turned clear and it was the
time of the meteor shower. What finally clinched
it was my taking back that globe, juggling it with
four or five pebbles I picked up, then sneaking it
onto his shoulder without his seeing.*

*He gasped. He was a child for magic. My tricks
for Powhatan astonished the great chief into admi-
ration, or so I thought until he called for water to
wash his hands and feathers to dry them and then
had two great stones brought before him.*

*They dragged me to the stones and laid my
head between them. They were standing over me
with their clubs raised to beat out my brains when
a slight girl just coming into womanhood rushed*

forward and took my head in her hands. Her hands were warm and light.

I didn't know it then, but it was a test. The girl was Pocahontas, Powhatan's dearest daughter. He never intended to kill me: he would adopt me to command my magic. The next moment he had me wrapped in his great robe adorned with the shells and pronounced me a werowance: his son. It was my twenty-seventh birthday.

I went back to Jamestown with provisions and carried on there, steadily planting and tilling to provide a sufficiency, guiding and building until a new group of colonists arrived. Men too ignorant to be grateful found my rule harsh and pushed me aside. Then, by accident or treachery, a coal fell on the bag of gunpowder I carried at my side. It exploded and burned. I suffered a terrible hurt that destroyed my manhood. Maimed and limping, out of favor and sick at heart, I returned to England on the ship that had carried out the newcomers. I was twenty-nine.

Alex stopped reading.

"He was here," Ebbs said, her voice heavy with emotion. "On this bank. It gives me gooseflesh to think of it. Smith, *here.* But enough. Turn in."

18

OLD HANDS

After a week on the water Alex's and Chuck's complexions were darker, and their hands, water-wrinkled and soft at first, were hard from working the ropes and doing camp chores.

They'd had every kind of weather from cold squalls of cutting rain that felt like spears of ice to dry burning sun to steamy, bug-buzzing nights. Alex had followed Ebbs's cloud-checking routine, so the weather changes didn't surprise her, just the timing. She'd watched the barometer too, but it never said *when* things would turn. They'd practiced knot tying, coming about fast, leaning out when a strong breeze made the boat heel. Alex began to regard the boat as a kind of animal, something alive with its own rhythms and habits, likes and dislikes.

She found the river alive too. To Alex it was an

endless, undulating gray-green snake rippling along, its riffles and small waves shimmering like scales. It struck Alex that with Ebbs everything was alive: clouds, boat, river, winds, space.

There were places along the river where boaters could tie up for gasoline, milk, beer, cigarettes, and ice cream. Ebbs was always good for a vanilla cone. Jeep liked them so much that whenever a marina came in view he'd start barking. Alex got her to buy ketchup to spice up the space foods, told her she'd better plan on sending some up with the astronauts.

At night the crew would study the tide chart and the river maps. Ebbs pointed out landmarks to look for the next day—things Smith would have seen—as they ate their space-food dinners. Around the campfire their talk would run long and unguarded, confidential and all over the place, the way talk goes sometimes in the dark among people who've come to trust one another. Chuck tried to explain why he'd had so much trouble in school—"so many things are going through my head at the same time, I can't focus on just one"—and Alex why she liked flying so much—"being alone and above everything, like

I'm in charge of it all." Ebbs told them she'd wanted to be a doctor, started medical school but caught TB from one of the cadavers she was dissecting, and had to quit. When she went back it was to study nutrition.

A couple of times they woke up to a silken world of mist, the fog fragrant with earth and river smells. Later, as the sun burned off the silver, the air took on the aroma of growing greens and flowers. Ebbs loved those mists, but she wouldn't set out until they lifted for fear of getting rammed. Except for maybe missing a good going-out ebb tide, it usually didn't matter much because until the sun warmed the air there was little wind anyway. The big boats, though, were on the river day and night, calling out with their powerful musical horns—wonderful sounds heard on shore, Alex discovered, terrifying if you were low on the water.

If anyone was around where they landed, Ebbs would ask permission to camp. Some nights they'd camped in soft pockets of tall grass and reeds, once on a muddy patch of raw red clay, another night in a stand of oaks that looked like feathers. Once, in a squall, they'd slept on board, Chuck in the cockpit fiddling with his radio, Alex with Ebbs up on deck, the girl tied down in her slicker with Jeep tight beside her as the boat pitched and the wind made the shrouds hum and moan and sometimes scream like fighting cats as the halyards slapped against the mast.

That night, all Alex could think about was having to pee, but she was too embarrassed to make Ebbs crawl out from under her tarp to untie her, so she lay there, twisting this way and that, afraid she'd fall asleep and wet herself. It was a terrible night. The next day they had to wear their wet clothes to dry them out.

Their last night on the river they tied up by a pine grove. It was warm and damp. They didn't bother putting up the tents.

Supper was another round of Ebbs's space food. "Turkey with dressing," Ebbs said.

"Doesn't taste like turkey," Chuck said, wrinkling his nose. "Tastes more like yesterday's beans."

"No, I think it's pretty close," Ebbs said, thoughtfully sniffing the bite on her fork. "Anyway, you heard last night how Smith and his crew were starving when they explored around here. He prided himself on equipping his expeditions with everything they'd need, but he overlooked nets—a big mistake because these waters are full of fish. Smith's people saw them in the shallows and tried to scoop them up in their frying pan. No luck.

"It was a fish that gave Smith the hurt that almost killed him. Standing in the shallows, he saw a big flat one glide by. He took out his dagger and stabbed it in the back. It turned and whipped him with its stingray tail—a barbed spike charged with poison. 'My arm swoled up the size of my thigh,' he wrote. Then it turned black. He was delirious, sick and dying, when they gave him some potion—he doesn't say what—and he survived to eat that ray fish.

"I wish we knew what the potion was that saved him. He should have said, but maybe he didn't know. Apothecaries—those were the druggists in those days—were real secretive, like pill makers today. We need to do better sharing what we know. After all, we've inherited for free most of what we see and use—everything from hybridized grains to sailboats to penicillin to radar. It's all part of the common store."

Dessert was the oranges Ebbs fished out of the bilge.

"But they're dirty," Alex complained, shaking some scum off of hers.

"They're OK," Ebbs said. "The cool water's kept them fresh, and their skin keeps 'em clean inside, like bananas and hard-boiled eggs. They're safe so long as you're careful how you peel them."

Alex peeled hers very carefully.

"For a special treat when we get to Tangier, I've got these coconuts," Ebbs said, hauling one up out of the hold. "Pete loves 'em. What you do is, you jam the point of your knife into these eyes to get at the milk and suck it out. Very nutritious. When they're empty we'll whack 'em open with the hatchet and eat the meat. Folks in the South Pacific can go for two or three days on a coconut."

As they licked orange juice from their fingers Ebbs showed Alex on the sea chart how they'd sail the next day, out across the upper bay. Working with the dividers from seamark to seamark, Alex figured the distance at seventeen miles. Ebbs had said it was close to twenty. Alex asked herself if she'd missed one of the small lantern-shaped symbols on the chart. She went back and checked. She had. *What if I miss one out there?*

Up to now they'd been on the river, never far from shore. Alex knew she could swim to the bank if she had to. Tomorrow, though, it was going to be all open water.

Chuck was crouched in front of his field radio. It looked like a thick, square suitcase covered in heavy dark green canvas against seawater and rain. Only the gleaming antenna showed what it was. He'd unsnapped the flap over the controls and was listening through headphones to what he could pick up from Wallops and anybody else transmitting within range.

"There's a lot of ship talk back and forth," he reported. "Coast Guard and weather stuff, pilots announcing bearings, and a lot of gibberish that must be navy stuff in code to keep it from the spies. Or maybe it's spies talking! Boy, if I could pick up one of *them*! I bet they're transmitting to Russian subs off the coast."

"A few years ago you might have picked up a German submarine," Ebbs said. "Hitler's U-boat 1105 was operating around here, the *Black Panther*. Took a while, but we finally got her. Not before she'd sunk a couple of tankers, though."

The moon was full, "the sun of the wolves," Ebbs said. There were frog calls, insects' churring, now and then the sound of something hitting the water. There was a slight breeze, almost enough to keep off the mosquitoes. The katydids were big and noisy, but they didn't bite.

Propped up against a vine-covered pine, Alex looked out into the bay. There were flickering channel lights, now and then the brief loom of a ship cutting a phosphorescent swath. A spotlight on the opposite shore caught patterns of ripples on the water.

A river is never silent. The water gurgles sounded like ragged breathing interrupted sometimes by slaps against the shore. It smelled of life. Ebbs told Alex that at its mouth the Potomac is about ten miles wide.

Ebbs and Chuck came over and sat down beside Alex. "This place is called Smith Point," Ebbs said. "Remember that boy, T, in the Smith painting? Well, T saved Smith's life here once with his hat. They'd been ambushed. The natives had Smith cornered when T put his hat up on a stick and started waving it around, yelling as loud as he could. That little distraction got Smith out of his hole."

Suddenly Jeep started barking. He stopped mid-yip, squealed, then began a long yowl that sent them running for the flashlights. A minute later he came whimpering into the firelight, his muzzle stuck with quills. Chuck and Alex spent the next hour holding him down while Ebbs dug out a dozen dirty black points barbed like fishhooks. He squealed when she scrubbed the raw places with rubbing alcohol. "Poor dog," Ebbs murmured. "VB would sympathize. When his first big test rocket blew up, the general in charge turned away saying, 'So you learn, Wernher, it is not so easy to tickle the porcupine.'"

19

At Sea

It was first light. Alex was dreaming and drifting, half-asleep, half-awake, when the sound of a hummingbird working a dark orange trumpet vine blossom just overhead snapped her alert. It sounded like a giant wasp. The bird was the size of her thumb, its beak stitching fast among the flowers like a long black needle, its wings invisible. It never stopped to rest. It was so fast, so slight and magical it made her smile. A squirrel began dropping chips of the green pinecone he was gnawing. The sky was streaked with pink like the inside of a shell. Low-flying birds skimmed over water that looked like it had been combed in two directions at once. Dew had caught in the spiders' webs in the grass, making them glow like pewter weavings.

Crows calling and crying roused Jeep. His muzzle was swollen, his nose parched. He'd had a bad night, dozing and whimpering, too pained even to push his way to the foot of Alex's bag, where he usually slept.

Alex wet a cloth from her canteen and bathed the dog's nose. Ebbs produced a can of chicken broth. Alex spooned it into Jeep's mouth sip by sip.

Ebbs hustled them through breakfast, each one mixing his own bowl of cereal with hot water. The cereal was the blend of dried grains called Meals for Millions that Ebbs had fed the refugees in Europe. The formula was one part cereal to six parts boiling water, then you shook on powdered milk. Busy tending to Jeep, Alex forgot the one cereal to six waters proportion. She mixed hers one to two parts, like oatmeal. There was tepid coffee with cocoa and sweetened condensed milk; then they waded out to the boat, Ebbs carrying Jeep paws up like he was a baby. "Next landfall, Tangier Island!" Ebbs called as Alex hauled up the anchors.

Alex had never been at sea before. Looking out over the open water, she couldn't see anything. She shivered with what she told herself was excitement.

Once they were under way, the morning sun glared off the water. The three sailors looked like desert travelers with smears of charcoal under their eyes and the hats and long-sleeved shirts Ebbs made them wear. Jeep groaned and nursed his hurt in his hammock under the deck.

Alex began to feel thirsty.

The water's emptiness made her uneasy. She wished she had something to do, like climbing a tree. She figured if you're not in the stern holding the tiller and running things, sailing's a waste of time—unless, of course, that's the only way to get where you're going. She decided the sailing life wasn't for her. She looked down at Jeep and nodded. The dog wagged feebly.

Between sessions of leaning out when Ebbs ordered it, Alex pumped and marked their course on the chart from seamark to seamark. Then she glanced at the barometer mounted on the cockpit cowling. "Hey, Ebbs!" she shouted. "The barometer's falling."

"Right!" Ebbs called back, glancing at the sky. "Weather's coming."

Over the next hour the wind changed quarters, opposing now as strongly as it had favored them before. Ebbs tacked this way and that, battling the onrush, spume swishing over the bow and gunnels as she worked the lurching winds to their advantage. They were all leaning out a lot now. It was a rough ride under fast-moving clouds, first mares' tails, then the slower, ominous low cumulus.

Chuck called over. "Hey, Alley! How far from Tangier to Wallops?"

Ebbs shook her head. "Can't do it, Chuck. Can't sail there in this. Anyway, Wallops is off-limits. No civilian boat can land there."

"OK, so never mind sailing to it," Chuck countered, "but as the crow flies, straight line from Tangier to Wallops, Alley, how far?"

Alex studied the map and worked the dividers. "Maybe thirty miles," she answered. "Seventeen over water, then maybe twelve across the peninsula, over the bridge to Chincoteague, then to the channel next to Wallops. But I don't see any bridge to Wallops."

"There isn't one," Ebbs snapped. "Put it out of your mind, Chuck. For security they keep it remote. The engineers and army folk live there in Quonset huts with no weekends off. You fly in or go by boat. No one is allowed to visit without prior authorization. It's a military installation—they're testing missile rockets there, so they're real edgy about spies and saboteurs. They've got armed guards all over the place."

Chuck frowned. "So we'll be watching the launch from thirty miles away? Heck! You can't see anything from that far, and anyway there'll be land humped up between us and them, so we won't see the tracking radar at all."

"If you're watching at the moment of liftoff you'll see the flame," Ebbs said, "maybe even get a glimpse of the rocket itself before you hear it. It's like a big rolling thunderclap."

"Yeah, but the tracking stuff," Chuck pressed, "the radar—we won't be able to see that."

"No."

"What does it look like?"

"Two saucers angled up, each as big across as a man," Ebbs said. "They're called Dopplers. They measure how fast the rocket's rising and track its direction. A technician stands beside each dish aiming it with a hand crank as the craft rises, *if* it rises. It's dangerous work. If the rocket fails on liftoff the technicians risk getting hurt. Some have."

Alex handed Chuck the map. He was fidgety as he studied it. "We could get closer, Ebbs," he said. "A lot closer. Like, we could go over to the peninsula and put in at Crisfield."

"Could," said Ebbs, "but Tangier's where we're headed."

"How do folks get to the mainland from Tangier?" Chuck asked.

"Most take the mail boat," Ebbs said.

"Does it go every day?" Chuck asked.

"Every day except Sunday. It's the island's lifeline, brings in news, batteries, gasoline, everything."

"Today's Saturday," Chuck said. "The launch is maybe tomorrow?"

"Maybe," said Ebbs. "I hear it might be the new rocket. They don't make it public, but they always cut back the mainland's power beforehand. When I called Pete from the marina to say we were heading out, he said Crisfield Harbor had gone dark to send extra out to Wallops. I know what you're thinking, Chuck, but put it out of your mind. Remember our deal: no more dumb moves. I'm working on our plan. Don't mess it up."

20

Rescue!

The wind had shifted again. The water was making a whapping sound against the *No Name*'s hull as she tacked and staggered a zigzag course through the bay's chop, a mile this way, a mile that to make a half mile toward Tangier. The land they'd left was a faint green line now. Alex couldn't make out the island. It was all empty, just sky and water, no left or right. *Lost in space, just like Ebbs said.*

The sky was beginning to look like curdled milk. The boat was yawing, rolling from side to side in the heavy waves. Alex had been drinking a lot of water. She figured it was the Meals for Millions getting even. Now she was feeling queasy. "I don't feel good," she announced.

Suddenly, like out of a bilge pump, the Meals for Millions surged up out of Alex. Without thinking, she bent over the side to throw up just as Ebbs yelled, "Coming about! Watch the boom!" Alex didn't hear. The boom went swinging like a bat across the deck. It caught Alex in her life vest, whacking her overboard.

She didn't know what hit her. Shocked by the blow and the sudden cold water, she gagged on vomit and salt water as her face, hands, and legs caught fire from some oozy, stringy stuff in the water—jellyfish! She tried to rub off the slimy, burning strands, but the more she touched, the more she burned. It was going all over her body. She was terrified, drowning in fire, trying to scream but couldn't—she was choking. The boat was moving away fast. It was all dark waves and emptiness around.

Ebbs tossed out a line as Chuck and Jeep dived in. It took a while for Ebbs to maneuver the *No Name* back to where Alex was paddling. Ebbs fished them all out, stung and dripping.

"Good timing, that jettison," Ebbs announced as she daubed Alex with a paste of baking soda. "Your up-chuck, I mean. Had you been sitting up, the boom would have sent your head off like a baseball."

Ebbs took off her poncho and wrapped Alex in it. It was warm. Alex felt better. *Nausea's the worst,* she thought. Worse than the burn of the jellyfish, even. She was still wet and cold, but she wasn't green anymore.

Ebbs looked up and pointed. "There it is, that smudge over there. That's Tangier."

At first the island appeared to rise up out of the water, but as they got closer it looked like they were higher and it was sinking, little humps of land and squares of buildings and thin things sticking up.

"This is the tricky part," Ebbs said as they got close. "The winds go all over the place, and the shore currents turn into swirls and eddies like whirlpools. We don't want to come crashing in."

They didn't. She brought them in without a bump. They docked near the mail boat. There were worn-looking fishing boats tied up close by, skiffs, some larger sailboats.

A couple of men were wheeling drums of diesel off the *Captain Sam;* others were stowing gear in a locker on the wharf. It was one in the afternoon. There didn't seem to be anybody else around.

They staggered over to Pete's shack like they were still on the boat's rocking deck. Even Jeep lurched like an old sailor.

Pete's place was a weathered shingle cottage behind a forest of sunflowers gone to seed, their browned lower leaves looking like ragged patches on skinny legs. Boat parts, driftwood, rusty chain, and some old anchors were piled around the door.

"Hello!" Pete said as they groped their way in. He gave Ebbs a hug. Coming in from the outside brightness, it was hard for Alex to see much at first. There was a hint of kerosene and good food smells.

As her eyes adjusted, Alex made out a short, barefoot man, square faced, with curly red hair and large gray eyes. She recognized him—he was the man in the photograph on Ebbs's card table. *Spy training pays off again,* she thought. *Now to find out who he is.*

"Sit down, eat, and tell all," Pete ordered.

Jeep looked up hopefully, his big tail fanning up dust fogs.

"You got something for him?" Alex asked.

"How about some of what we're having?" Pete said.

"Yeah, sure."

Jeep downed his bowl in two gulps as the others ate warm slabs of buttered bread and emptied bowls of Pete's own make stew. After ten days of Ebbs's stuff, real food tasted great.

"So you're the downstream crew," Pete said as they all stretched back happily, bellies full. "I'm her crew for the upstream run. You get her war stories around the campfire?"

"You mean about getting von Braun?" Alex asked.

"There's that, but what followed was what she got decorated for—what they called 'the hidden war.'"

"Lay off, Pete," Ebbs said, shaking her head.

"Tell us!" Alex and Chuck said in one voice so firmly it made Jeep woof.

"They put her in charge of feeding the refugees," Pete explained. "They knew there'd be a lot, but they never guessed ten million. With everything all torn up in Europe, and our own supplies stretched, it was touch and go, but if those people had starved it would have been worse than Hitler. I was her driver. She sent us tearing around all over, hunting stuff, moving stuff, even stealing where she thought the army had too much. She had a nose for where food was, sent out spies to find it. She even got two famous German cooks to put their names on a new recipe for corn—that's what we had the most of—but the Germans said corn was pigs' food and wouldn't eat it. The name she made up for it didn't mention it was corn—she called it by the names of those two famous cooks and made it popular. That alone probably saved a million lives. When it was all over they made up a special decoration for her," Pete said, beaming at Ebbs. "And let me tell you, she earned it!"

"Enough!" Ebbs ordered. Alex had never seen her blush before, didn't know she could.

Chuck was restive. "We gotta go exploring. We've been cooped up on that boat for more than a week; we've gotta get out and move around. I feel like I'm bobbing."

"Don't get lost," Pete said. "Tangier's a mile wide and three long, and it's filled with Methodists."

Chuck and Alex ambled down Tangier's spine. Circling back, they found themselves at the main dock. They didn't have a plan. Alex couldn't have said why they'd headed over toward the mail boat, but there she was. It was a warm afternoon. Folks were snoozing off their lunches. There was no one around.

The *Captain Sam*'s lifeboat was hanging above the deck under a canvas wrap. *Just like in Smith's journal,* Alex thought. She knew what Chuck was thinking.

"Alley!" he whispered as he pointed to the lifeboat. "If we can get up in there we can ride over to the mainland, maybe get to Wallops—just like John Smith did when *he* first took off."

Alex opened her mouth to say no like she'd promised Ebbs, but the chance was too tempting. It seemed like all of a sudden they were following Smith's plan.

Alex nodded. "Jeep too?"

Chuck frowned and shook his head. "No. Leave him. He'll find his way back to Pete's."

Alex folded her arms across her chest. "If I go, he goes."

Chuck's face darkened. "Then I'll go alone."

Alex flinched like she'd been hit.

"I take it back," Chuck said quickly. "We'll all go."

He boosted Alex up so she could loosen the cords securing the canvas cover. When there was enough of a hole, Chuck pushed her in. Nobody noticed when he lifted up the big brown dog and then hoisted himself in.

They lay down inside. A little later there were voices, yells, ship horns tooting, rumbles and churning and the smell of diesel smoke as the ship pulled away from the dock. It settled into a long drumming and up-and-down rocking as she crossed the channel to the mainland. Anybody looking up from the *Captain Sam*'s deck as they went along wouldn't have noticed anything strange, save for what appeared to be a panting dog's muzzle sticking out from under the canvas as the lifeboat rocked on its davits.

21

Suspicious Characters

The stowaways waited hot and sweating in their hide-hole until they didn't hear any more voices. Then Alex pushed Jeep aside and lifted the canvas enough to peek out. She didn't see anyone on the ship's deck. The wharf where they'd tied up was a whole lot bigger than the one at Tangier, with boats for charter fishing, luxury yachts, a launch with FBI painted on the side in big black letters, fuel tanks, ice machines, a big refrigerator with a bluefish and a crab painted on it, old tires wound with rope for boat buffers, crates, nets, coils of rope, crab traps, a gas pump, water hydrants. The *Captain Sam* was just one of the larger ships moored there. Alex could hear voices, people loading ice, wheeling cargo down the planked dock, nobody close by.

"Let's go!" she whispered. As she climbed out she

looked across the water. On the nearby island she spotted what she figured must be the radio masts on Wallops.

"It's over there!" she exclaimed.

When they got to the road Chuck put out his thumb. Her dad had warned Alex about hitchhiking. It was one of the few things Chuck did that she'd never attempted.

A boy driving an old pickup piled high with bushels of tomatoes waved a suntanned arm and pulled over.

"Where you headed?" His accent was soft and musical.

"Wallops," said Chuck. "Close as we can get."

"Get in, then. It's gonna be some crowded, but we can do it."

The boy was tall and gangly. His shirt was an old plaid so worn and tomato-stained the pattern didn't show anymore. He didn't take up much room. Alex fit in the middle, her legs straddling the gearshift. Chuck sat on the outside with Jeep in his lap.

Alex thought the boy looked familiar.

The jalopy started up with a shudder.

"So you're goin' to watch the launch, huh? I can drop you by Chincoteague Channel. That's as good a watching place as any."

"Thanks," Chuck said as he sat tensed on the edge of the Ford's worn seat. "That's the closest?"

"It's the best for watching," the boy replied. "Wallops

sits out there a mile, mile and a half from most everything 'cepting the marshes, which is why they chose it. Used to be a hunting preserve. Ducks is still there, but the hunters ain't, so now when they set them rockets off there must be a million birds scares up."

Alex stared at him. She thought he was handsome and she liked the easy way he talked. The more she looked at him, though, the surer she was she'd seen him before.

"But what's closest?" Chuck pressed.

The boy rubbed his face a little and stuck out his jaw. Alex noticed the faint beginning of red beard. "Closest I reckon is Ruther's Point off Chicken House Road. Couples go out there but not to watch the launches on account you don't get a direct view."

Chuck was nodding. "Sounds right for us, though, being closest."

"So you all want to go out to the Point?"

"Yeah," said Chuck. "But we don't want to put you out. . . ."

"It's on my way," the boy replied cheerfully. "The cannery is just beyond where I'll drop you. I do hauling for the farmers, five cents a bushel for these tomatoes—loading, hauling, and unloading."

He pointed to a shoebox full under the seat. "Try one. There's salt in the corner."

It was the tastiest tomato Alex had ever eaten.

"You work or go to school?" the boy asked.

Alex started to say "school" when Chuck spoke up. "I'm looking for work," he replied. "How about you?"

"I do this. Quit school to help my mom. My dad was killed in the war." He paused. "It's my own truck, '26 T-Model. Rebuilt her myself," he added proudly.

"Oh yeah?" said Chuck. "I rebuilt a war surplus jeep. You really get to know 'em that way, feel everything."

"Yeah!" piped up Alex. "Even the spark. He tested the dynamo on me—knocked me down!"

"*That* was dumb!" the boy exclaimed, sticking out his hand to Alex. "Name's TJ. First name sounds like Tolliver, second's Jester. What's yours?"

"Alex. This here's my brother Chuck and our dog, Jeep."

TJ looked over at Chuck. "How old are you?"

"Seventeen. You?"

"Fifteen. I'll be sixteen in September."

"They let you drive at fifteen down here?" Chuck asked.

"Agricultural license," TJ explained. "Special tags on the truck. Can't run it out of the county."

He glanced over at Alex. "Bet you can't spell my first name."

She tried: "T-o-l-l-i-v-e-r."

TJ snorted. "Nowhere *close*! It's T-a-l-l-i-f-e-r-r-o—

a real old name around here. In what they say's the first cemetery on Chincoteague, the state historical people found a stone with a *T* carved on it real rough, so maybe it's the first Talliferro under there. I run my finger in the letter, it made my hair go up, so I think he's kin. Over to Snow Hill there's Revolutionary War stones with 'Talliferro' spelled out, and a Civil War dead is buried behind our house. My dad was a Talliferro too, but they buried him over in Europe."

He frowned and gripped the wooden wheel.

"When was that?" Alex demanded. "When was that first *T* person here?"

TJ gave her a surprised look. "The historian folks who came out from Baltimore said the cemetery is from 1620, so I figure some time before that. Why?"

"Because maybe you're kin to Captain John Smith's servant," Alex said excitedly. "Our friend Ebbs has got a painting of Captain Smith with him in it. She's kin to Captain Smith, and has all this stuff he wrote in his journal too—we've been reading it, so we know a lot about him. You look like the boy in the picture. In the journal his name begins with what looks like a *T,* but the rest is too smudged to make out, so maybe Smith left him and he ended up here."

"Could be the same one," TJ said, nodding as he

squinted and set his mouth. "I wanna see that picture. Where is it?"

"Our friend Ebbs has it," Alex said, pleased to have his attention. "She's related to Smith, like I said—and maybe you are to T, so you two gotta meet."

"Gotta!" TJ agreed.

"You guys got an old name too?" he asked, turning to Chuck.

"My first name is," Chuck replied, fingering the worn gold ring with the beveled blue stone his mother had given him. "It says Carlus inside, 'Charles' in Latin. My last name they just hung on me. Alley here, though, her last name is Hart. She owns it OK."

"Huh," said TJ. "What happened to your folks, Chuck?"

"No idea, but the thing about names is, you could be anybody, right? You could call yourself Adam if you wanted to, and who'd be the wiser?"

TJ bunched up his mouth a little. "Never thought of it that way, but what would you do for papers?"

"Papers?"

"Birth certificate, stuff like that."

"Forge one easy as pie. Spies do it all the time like counterfeiters fake money. We've read stories about 'em."

They rode along silent for a while, the engine clunking

away with a hollow sound as whiffs of exhaust and dust swirled in the cab.

TJ spat out the window.

Finally he asked, "What kind of work you want to do, Chuck?"

"Radio, radar, maybe something on Wallops."

Alex fidgeted. She wanted TJ to ask *her* questions.

Chuck studied TJ's face. Alex knew what was coming.

"We've got to get out there," Chuck said, pointing out over the water. "At least I do."

"Me too!" said Alex.

"Wallops? You can't," said TJ. "It's all classified, military, missiles and all. Real secret."

"I know," said Chuck, "but I've got to go see the radar dishes."

"*We,*" said Alex. "We're both students of it."

TJ frowned and half turned to Chuck. "Go easy, mister. You're talking suspicious. That stuff you said about names and forgeries? Folks around here get wind of that and they'll think you're dangerous. I'd turn you in if I thought you was, but watch how you talk. We're all real protective about what goes on over there, what with the Russians and all. There's warning posters in the post office."

TJ slowed the truck and pulled over at the mouth of a rutted track lined with oyster shells.

"This is you. Point's about a half mile down. Can't drive you in on account of this load. All that's Wallops over there," he said, waving at the lump of gray beyond the pines. "Good luck. You end up needing supper or a place to sleep, we're the corner house, Jesters and Main. There's a sign out front, Jester's Used Books—my mom's business."

"Thanks, TJ," Alex said. "I'm going to get you together with our friend Ebbs. You've gotta be the same family as T."

"Do that," TJ said. "I'm real curious."

Jeep was already nosing around in the stinking marsh when Alex and Chuck waved off the pickup.

They walked down to the Point and looked out at Wallops. They could see the launch site shapes and structures where the lights were.

"No wonder they had to cut the mainland's power," Chuck muttered. "Still daylight but they've got it lit up like New York City."

22

WALLOPS

The channel looked to be a mile across at least.

"I'm hungry," Alex announced.

Mosquitoes settled on them like a cloud.

They were standing on a patch of dried mud patterned like cracked glaze. Jeep was snuffling around a sodden hulk half-sunk in water. Chuck waved his hands like windshield wipers to keep the bugs off his face.

"So, Alley, how do we get over there?"

"There's boats at that place we passed on the road coming here," she said. "We'll rent one—tell 'em we're going fishing."

As they crunched back up the white-shelled track Chuck felt in his pockets for money. He fingered up a dime and a quarter. "This is it, Alley—all I've got."

It was dim inside Cousin Marge's. It smelled of

cigarettes, stale beer, fish, and frying. They had enough for two mugs of soup and a coffee. The hard round crackers and horseradish paste on the table were free, so they filled up on those as Chuck emptied the sugar bowl into the cup of coffee he shared with Alex. Soon as they finished the coffee the cream went into the mug for Jeep. The dog worked the mug like a hummingbird going at a honeysuckle blossom: not a splash, not a drop wasted.

The jukebox was going in the corner. Two couples sat in separate booths. Three men were hunched together over their beers in another. By studying their shoes and boots Alex worked out that the men had come in the boats outside, the couples had come in the cars.

The men ordered another round. They were just warming up.

"We'll have to borrow from them, Chuck," Alex said, indicating with her head the men in the booth.

Chuck paid and they went out, sauntering like tourists down the dock. The skiff at the far end had an outboard. So did the newer-looking dory, but that one could be seen from Marge's window.

"The skiff, right?" Alex said as they moved down the dock.

Chuck swung into it smooth and easy like he owned it. Alex jumped in lightly, dragged in the dog, then lifted the painter from the piling and pushed off hard as Chuck

primed the motor, put the throttle to low, and set the choke. Three pulls and it caught, spitting and spluttering. Acting like they were in no hurry, Chuck eased off the choke until he'd brought the motor to a steady purr, then powered it up to a roar and headed out across the channel. They didn't look back. They couldn't hear anything over the motor.

Chuck didn't aim for the lights. He pointed them toward the far end of the island, the boat going *flapaflapaflap* as she pounded across the waves. There was fishing gear

at his feet and a gray felt hat like their dad's, only worn
and stained. Alex put it on. "Disguise," she said.

The oars stowed against the gunwales were banged
up, the handles worn with use. None of the fishing gear
was fancy sportsman's stuff. Alex felt bad about taking
from a workingman, but then she figured whoever owned
the boat would get it back soon one way or another—
they weren't going far.

Just then the engine staggered a few beats and
died.

Chuck checked the tank and shook his head at Alex. "Dry."

The shore was about a block away now. They were close enough to make out trees, branches, and the tall fence festooned with red, white, and blue signs.

Thinking *jellyfish,* Alex asked, "Do we swim it?"

Chuck shoved an oar into the water. Halfway in it stuck in mud.

"No, it's not deep. We can walk it. Keep your shoes on; the shells are sharp."

Chuck jumped in, gasping at the cold shock. "The bottom's firm enough. Your turn!"

Twisting around, keeping her hands on the gunnels, Alex swung herself in, panting and blowing as the cold hit. With a big drenching splash Jeep dived in beside her.

Alex kept the hat on.

Jeep swam on before them. Chuck half towed Alex until it was shallow enough for her to clamber on her own, mud and muck sucking at her shoes. They met up with no jellyfish.

There was a narrow margin of marsh weed and ooze, then the tall Cyclone fence with strands of barbed wire flecked with blades strung in swirls on spokes leaning out along the top.

Alex figured she and Chuck could make it over somehow, but what about Jeep? They couldn't leave him.

They were stuck: no way in and no way to get back. The boat had drifted out of sight by now. *Ebbs will kill me,* Alex thought. *I was supposed to say no to stuff like this.*

Every fifty feet were red warning signs on the fence: DANGER! NO TRESPASSING. HIGH SECURITY AREA. U.S. GOVERNMENT PROPERTY. PENALTY FOR TRESPASSING: FINE AND IMPRISONMENT.

A flat, slow-paced loudspeaker voice droned in the distance, the breeze and water noise blotting out the words.

Near where they stood the fence was humped up over a rock the size of a large wastebasket. High tides and storm wash had loosened it.

Exploring the shoreline they found a heavy piece of driftwood. They dragged it back to the rock, levered the rock aside enough to make a slither hole, pushed Jeep through, then squirmed under themselves.

"Wallops!" Chuck whooped. "We made it! I've got that great taste in my mouth, Alley! This is *big*!"

Their faces were streaked, their bodies covered in greasy, dead-smelling mud.

Jeep shook himself, sending clots of mud and sand flying. Everything except his muzzle was smeared and splattered. The only other unmuddied thing about them was the hat Alex had managed to keep dry and now pulled low over her head.

"Ha!" Chuck exulted. "Wish I had a picture, Alley! So here's our plan. We're Captain Smith going to meet the Turks. We're going to walk toward the lights. When we get close enough to be seen you're gonna put that hat up on a stick so if they start shooting that's what they'll hit first."

Shooting? Then Alex remembered what Ebbs and TJ had said about security on the island—"armed guards." She caught her breath. She'd been scared before—caught in her spy tree when a thunderstorm came up, knocked overboard earlier that day—but this was worse: soldiers might be *shooting* at her?

Chuck doesn't care, she thought as he kept talking away.

"Then we're going to start marching like we're going to a camp inspection: hut-two-three-four, hut-two-three-four, and, and"—he was getting more and more worked up—"and we're gonna be singing—yeah!—*singing*! 'Halls of Montezuma'—singing it as loud as we can. We're gonna get caught—we *want* to get caught, OK? But they won't shoot if we come on like that. When they get us, let me do the talking. It's gonna be scary, you're gonna be scared, me too, but whatever they ask or threaten just pretend they're all standing around in dirty underwear, embarrassed and wishing they could get away. Got it? Once they see you're a girl we'll be OK. They'll never shoot a girl."

Gonna be scared? Alex thought as she tried to wipe the mud away from her tickling nose. The back of her hand was even muddier than her face. Her knuckle smeared on a clown's mustache. *Underwear? They'll never shoot a girl?*

They started out. Chuck picked up a long stick, forked at the end. "Perfect!" he exclaimed. "When I say to, perch the hat on it so it rides level and hold it up high as a tall man. A decoy!"

Like what T did for Smith, Alex thought. *Hope it works again.*

"Keep control of Jeep," Chuck ordered. "Don't let him get excited and lunge or bark or anything. It's all a game, right? Play it like a game. We're gonna see that rocket and the radar!"

It was dark. Lightning bugs flickered. They made their way toward the launch site lights until they came to a long stretch of paving painted with yellow bars. In the darkness they could make out several small airplanes parked off to one side.

"A landing strip!" Chuck said in a hushed voice. "You know what, Alley? Maybe I'll fly us out of here in one of those after the launch—do a Captain Smith escape!"

It was too dark for Alex to see Chuck's face, but she knew he meant it.

The loudspeaker was clear now, the voice slow and methodical as it reported the launch protocols: "Procedure thirty-two." Pause. "Check. Procedure thirty-three."

Alex was shivering but she wasn't cold. Jeep rambled and sniffed, marking territory as he went along.

They were skirting a lighted circle now, three sides of it a concrete baffle barrier with a clamshell roof pulled back. Suddenly, coming up on the open side, they could see the rocket. Alex forgot about being scared. She caught her breath. It was beautiful—shinier and more wonderful, more *alive* than anything in Ebbs's photographs, even though it was smaller than the V-2 in Ebbs's picture. The rocket was slender and straight-sided, the latticework gantry hugging it like a mother her child, a flag and USA in vertical black letters on the side, its gleaming white nose. The nose was wreathed in swirls of fog-like mist. The rocket was surrounded by a lot of machines and pipes and men scurrying around. It was like a giant white wasp in its cocoon, trembling, dangerous.

"Liquid oxygen or maybe coolant," Chuck said softly, pointing at the mist. "Put up the hat."

The loudspeaker droned on: "Procedure fifty." Pause. "Check. Procedure fifty-one."

Off to the right was a low cinder block box with a

few small rectangular openings, each the size of a shoe-box. "Flight control," Chuck whispered.

Then: "Look, Alex!" A few yards beyond were the big radar dishes they were looking for—the Dopplers.

"Oh, man," she sighed, all the air going out of her at once. They were like giant eyes, insect eyes, monster eyes for the towering white wasp.

A uniformed operator stood to one side of the clos-est radar dish, his hands resting on the aiming wheel he would use to keep the dish focused on the missile as it rose.

Alex couldn't help it. The hat on the stick began weaving and twitching.

The operator noticed and started yelling.

"Forward, march!" Chuck bawled.

They began moving toward the cinder block box, Chuck marching stiff and formal, Alex stumbling to get in step as Chuck roared out the song, Jeep striding along-side, tail up—

"From the Halls of Montezuma
To the shores of Tripoli
We fight our country's battles
In the air, on land, and sea . . ."

23

TO THE SHORES OF TRIPOLI

"Hey! *Halt!* What are you doing here?"

They stopped, Alex marching in place with Chuck now, singing with him as loud as she could to drown out her fear:

"From the Halls of Montezuma . . ." Stomp, stomp, stomp, stomp . . . *"To the shores of Tripoli . . ."*

A short, bullet-headed man and two others with pistols drawn circled around, blinding them with their flashlights. Alex put on the hat and pulled it down to shield her eyes. Then she reached out to steady Jeep.

"From the Halls of Montezuma . . ." Stomp, stomp, stomp, stomp . . .

"Shut up! Stop moving!"

Alex stood still.

"Take off his hat," Bullet Head ordered.

The soldier, a private, lifted it off and held it away from himself as if it were a rotten fish.

"She's a girl!" he exclaimed. "A kid."

"Give it back," Alexcried. "I borrowed it!"

Jeep growled as his ruff went up.

Bullet Head backed away. "You keep a holt of that dog!"

He turned to Chuck. "Who are you? Whaddya think you doing?"

Alex was shaking with excitement, but she wasn't scared now. It was just like they had planned. She felt like she was watching a play, except that she was also acting in the play and had no idea what her next lines were going to be.

"We-want-to-watch-the-launch," Chuck declared slowly in a loud, flat voice mocking the loudspeaker.

The private gave him a close look. "He's crazy."

"Like heck," said Bullet Head. "Fronts for commie spies. Pat 'em down!"

"Nothing on either one," the private said when he finished. "They don't seem to have a dime between them, Sarge, or anything else."

"Old commando trick," Bullet Head said. "Concealing identity. Take 'em over to the bunker."

"Launch procedure sixty-three. Check."

Chuck squeezed Alex's hand. " 'Matilda' this time."

As they started moving they began marching and singing again, louder than before—

"Waltzing Matilda . . ." Stomp, stomp, stomp, stomp. Jeep parading along beside them.

The flight control bunker was separated from the gantry by the blast shield. It was crowded with men in military uniforms and others in business suits with name tags and binoculars hung around their necks. Men in fatigues sat at control desks against the wall studying monitor screens and instruments.

As they entered, Jeep balked and looked up at Alex. They both smelled food.

"Launch procedure sixty-five. Check."

"We got intruders here!" Bullet Head yelled as he motioned to the private to push the captives in.

Everybody turned to stare.

"Launch procedure seventy. Check."

"Halt!"

As Alex and Chuck marched in place, flakes of caked mud fell onto the floor like they were shedding.

"Stand still!"

The captain looked about their father's age. He had pens and a slide rule stuck in his khaki shirt pocket. There were sweat stains under his arms. Alex took him for an engineer. He got their names, then studied them so closely Alex could feel his heat.

"What are you doing?" he asked.

"We want to watch the launch," Chuck said louder than he needed to. "We want to see the rocket go up and watch the radar working. I'm a student of space."

"Me too," Alex said.

"Where're you from?"

"Silver Spring, Maryland," Chuck answered.

"How'd you get here?"

Chuck kept answering. "Sailed down the Potomac from DC, then out to Tangier. This afternoon we caught the mail boat to Crisfield, hitched a ride to Chincoteague, and, uh, got ourselves over here."

"How?"

"Swam, waded."

"Sure. Who brought you over?"

Chuck shook his head. "Nobody."

"So you borrowed or stole a boat," the captain said, squinting at Chuck as if to understand him better.

"Launch procedure eighty-three. Check."

The captain shook his head like he was trying to clear it.

"Lieutenant," he ordered, "radio the Coast Guard to check around the island for the boat these folks used. Then get the FBI to send somebody over to collect 'em."

FBI! Alex felt a surge of panic. *Will they arrest us like spies in the newspapers?* She fought to stay calm.

The captain turned back to Chuck.

"How old are you?"

"Seventeen."

"And you?" he said to Alex.

"Twelve."

"You in school?"

Alex stood at attention and nodded like she'd seen prisoners do in the movies. "Sixth grade, sir! Parkside Elementary, sir! Silver Spring, Maryland, sir!"

The captain puckered back a smile. "Same as my daughter," he muttered. "And you?" he said to Chuck.

"I finished high school June a year ago. Blair. I started at Tech but had to leave. I've done the National Radio Institute course. I want to work with radar. . . ."

"Have you ever done anything like this before?"

"I've been picked up a couple of times for tres-passing."

"Seems to be your habit," the captain said. "Where?"

"Washington. Climbing the WTOP tower, checking the broadcast waves," Chuck said proudly. "Then trying out an airplane."

The captain's eyebrows went up. "Airwaves to air-planes to rockets. There's an escalating pattern here. Did you come alone—I mean, you and your sister?"

"Yes, sir," said Alex, determined to have a voice in things.

The lieutenant was talking on his radio nearby. Suddenly he was speaking louder: "Hart, I said. Hart. H-A-R-T. H-Harry, A-Alpha, R-Romeo, T-Tango. I said, see if you can get anything on them. Yeah, we got 'em here in custody. Come get them."

Chuck nudged Alex. "From now on," he whispered, "you're H-Harry, A-Alpha, R-Romeo, T-Tango."

Another officer came over to report to the captain. "Discovered where they got in, sir, and Coast Guard reports finding the boat they must have used. They were out looking for it. Belongs to Mr. Brownlowe on Chincoteague, reported missing a couple of hours ago. Folks saw two kids stealing it from Cousin Marge's."

"OK," said the captain. "Well, we're not going to

stop the launch on account of two muddy trespassers. But launch or no launch, I want a work detail out there right now securing that fence!"

"Launch procedure eighty-six. Check."

Bullet Head started pushing Alex and Chuck into a corner.

"Might as well let 'em watch," the captain called. "They worked hard enough to get here. And get 'em blankets. Wrap 'em up. Better yet, send 'em to the shower, Sarge. Laundry soap—the strongest you got! They're filthy! Get 'em to wash the dog too, and give 'em dry clothes."

Bullet Head's face fell. The captain read his mind. "You've got time, Sarge. Launch won't be for another twenty, thirty minutes."

When Bullet Head herded his prisoners back in they looked scrubbed and awkward, shuffling in baggy GI gear and boots too big. Jeep rushed around shaking himself dry in frenzied spasms, rubbing up against posts and table legs.

"Cap'n," Bullet Head called. "There's more pairs of those binoculars the contractor folks been passing out? These kids could use them."

"Go ask the gent over there," the captain answered, pointing to a man in a business suit. "He's been handing 'em out as souvenirs."

"Launch procedure one-hundred-fourteen. Check."

The food they'd smelled when they came in was set out on a table against the back wall. Jeep went over to it, wagging hard.

Bullet Head called to the captain again. "Dog's hungry, sir."

"So feed him. You kids hungry too?" the captain asked.

Alex and Chuck nodded.

"Launch procedure one-hundred-sixteen. Check."

"So eat."

The three of them were stuffing down hush puppies, fried oysters, and spicy crab cakes when suddenly Alex stiffened. A big man in coveralls came in with a couple of others. They looked like mechanics. The big one lit a cigarette as the captain joined them.

"Chuck! It's *him*!" Alex whispered. "VB's *here*."

Chuck squared his shoulders and took a deep breath.

"Sir!" he bellowed as loud as he could.

The room hushed. Everyone—including the big man—looked over.

"Herr Doktor von Braun! Ebbs sent me!"

24

MOON GIRL RISING

Von Braun came over. He stared at Chuck, then Alex, his blue eyes cold, probing.

"You," he said, pointing to Alex, "you, I know. You are Louise Hart's daughter, the one who watches for the weather balloons. You showed me your Moon Station. But who is this other one?"

"My brother."

"Ah. The inventor who does escapades," VB murmured as he studied Chuck closely. "You do not look related."

"We're not," Chuck said. "Thank you for the theodolite," he added.

Von Braun gave him a sharp look. "Do you use it?"

"All the time. We ditched the compass like you said."

VB nodded a little. "So what do you mean, Ebbs sent you? What do you do here?"

"She didn't *exactly*," Alex started to explain, but Chuck drowned her out.

"I'm a student of space," he said loudly. "I want to see the rocket and the radar. I want to help you. I want to see the launch and watch the Dopplers, see how they work tracking the rocket."

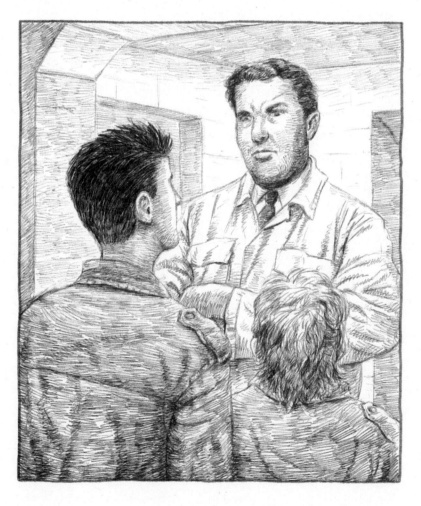

"Why?"

"I want to go up in one of your rockets. Out, I mean. Fly for you. Meanwhile, I want to make radar dishes."

VB's eyes narrowed. "Radar? Why radar?"

"Because I want to see what's coming at me."

"And Ebbs sent you to break in here and maybe get shot so you can see the radars?"

"It's not her fault!" Alex cried. "All she did was get us to Tangier in her sailboat. She said she'd heard they were testing rockets on Wallops and maybe there'd be a launch. We were going to watch from Tangier, but it's too far away—we wouldn't see anything—so we came over on our own. Ebbs didn't have anything to do with it."

Suddenly the loudspeaker blared, "Holding! Holding! Holding!"

"Sir!" a mechanic called, rushing up. "The coolant return line—it's plugged."

Von Braun and the others hurried out to the launch platform, Chuck and Alex following so close Bullet Head couldn't snatch them back.

A few minutes later von Braun and the engineers were huddled over a drawing of the valve. Alex and Chuck wormed in beside them.

"It's like the picture in my science book," Alex whispered. "It looks like one of the flaps in a person's heart that keeps pumped blood from flowing back."

Von Braun nodded. "So perhaps the valve is stuck shut?" he asked no one in particular.

The man who had given Alex and Chuck the binoculars stepped forward, the blood gone from his face.

"We tested and tested, sir, but I'll call and have another one sent up."

"Maybe it's just jammed," Chuck whispered. "Let's cut it out of the line and see. I can free it up if the problem's what I think—a bit of metal pinning the flap. We can clear it, then thread the repair back in."

Von Braun pinched his lips together and nodded. He turned to the captain. "The mechanics and plumbers on the base can cut out the section for us, yes?"

The captain shifted uncomfortably. "Uh, Doctor, doing that fix on the gantry while the rocket is sitting there live is risky. Even if we do it, if the line fails on ignition there could be an explosion. It would be safer to scrub the launch and replace the whole thing."

Von Braun's eyes were like steel drills. "Captain, I asked if we can do what this boy just described."

The captain reddened. "Cut out the valve section and then plumb it back in place? Yes, sir, we can do that."

Von Braun looked away. "Tonight we have a good launch window. Tomorrow, not so good . . . And your part," he said, turning to the ghastly-looking contractor, "we would get it—when?"

"We—we'll fly it right up from Texas," he stammered. "Have it here tomorrow afternoon, for sure."

Chuck locked eyes with von Braun. "What's to lose trying my fix?" he asked.

"What's to lose?" von Braun repeated slowly. "That's the big American idea, isn't it? Well, what's to lose is the explosion the captain is worried about, but *that* never enters your head any more than what you risked sneaking in here with her and maybe getting both of you killed."

Von Braun looked away again, then nodded and turned to the captain. "Do the fix. I take responsibility."

He turned to Chuck. "So we try it. Her official name is *Boojum,* but if our rocket goes up we call her the *What's to Lose.*"

"No, Doctor," Alex interjected. "She's the *Moon Girl,* and she's gonna fly just fine!"

It took a while to drain the broken line. Then the plumber began sawing. That didn't take long at all.

Von Braun took hold of the cut section as it came clear, held it up to the light, then bent down and tapped an end on the pavement. A sliver of metal fell out.

It took an hour for the mechanics to thread the four pipe ends and fit on the two connectors. At last, they had the piece threaded back in. The flight controllers slowly restored pressure to the line and tested it against back-flow. The valve worked; the repair joints held.

Von Braun smiled as he gave the signal. "Resume countdown at procedure one-hundred-forty-one."

When they cleared procedure 160, they pushed away the rocket's embracing gantry. *She's on her own now,* Alex thought. The official began the final countdown. Folks in the bunker bent over, cowering against the blast to come, but Alex didn't. When the voice said "Zero," von Braun pressed the large red IGNITE button. There was a blinding flash, then a shattering rolling roar that seemed to inhabit Alex and then felt like it was swallowing her as searing light blanketed everything. Alex squinted, holding her breath as she watched the rocket. For a long instant it seemed to hang trembling and uncertain above its bil-lowing motors. Then slowly, slowly, then faster and faster it rose in a shocking magnificence of swirling white flame like a bride preceding a long windblown train, Alex screaming and cheering as hard as she could.

Chuck's eyes were on the closest radar dish as the op-erator shielded his eyes from the glare with one hand and spun the aiming wheel with the other, pointing the dish as the missile rose like a glowing meteor.

"On course," came the voice over the loudspeaker as folks in the bunker applauded von Braun. Weak but exhilarated, Alex was somewhere between laughing and crying. *We did it,* she sobbed to herself. *We did it!*

Minutes later *Moon Girl* was all done with, the perfect flight over as her glowing hot core plopped into the Atlantic a hundred miles downrange with a burst of steam that must have cooked every jellyfish around.

It would be hours before there would be flight data for von Braun to study. For the moment he could breathe easy. Except for the matter of Chuck and Alex.

25

CHUCK'S GENIUS

Jeep rested comfortably, stuffed and tired at Alex's feet, as von Braun questioned the trespassers. "All in one day, with the dog, you two sail from Smith Point in Virginia out to Tangier Island, you meet a friend there and eat, then you stow away on the mail boat to Crisfield, then you hitchhike and eat again and steal a boat, then you run out of fuel and you wade ashore and break in here—our most secure missile base—singing and marching, and you do not get shot, they just give you soap and clothes and feed you *again* and give you binoculars? Is it possible?"

"It's what we did," Alex said proudly, "and on the way I got seasick and the boom knocked me into the water and I got burned by jellyfish. But it wasn't Ebbs who sent us here," she added, looking over at Chuck. "Getting to Wallops was *our* idea."

"Mine mostly," Chuck said.

The FBI launch arrived with a roar and a great splashing wake to take the interlopers off the island. It was a sleek mahogany runabout. As it docked, the tied-up navy boats nearby rocked like drab pigeons next to a peacock. The plainclothes agents were armed, certain they were collecting spies. The one in charge was shocked when he saw his prisoners.

"A pair of strays," the captain explained, giving the chief a bland smile. "Landed here by accident. Out fishing, ran out of gas, came ashore at the closest place, which is here. No breach of security, nothing criminal, no record. All we need you for is to give 'em a ride back to Chincoteague."

"That's it? Them?" the chief asked, incredulous.

"Like I told you, these kids landed here by accident," the captain repeated. "Now you've got to get 'em out of here."

"Get 'em to where?" the agent asked disgustedly.

"To TJ's," Alex said. "Call him. He lives at Jester's Used Books, Jesters and Main, Chincoteague."

Alex and Chuck stood with von Braun while the agent called and got directions from TJ, then waited and started speaking with someone else. They could hear a deep woman's voice as the agent began stammering, "Yessum. Yessum. Yessum."

"Ask if Captain Ebbs is there," von Braun ordered.

The agent jerked around, disconcerted to hear von Braun's heavy accent.

"Captain Ebbs," von Braun repeated. "Is she there?"

"Are you Captain Ebbs?" the agent asked the woman on the line.

She was.

"Give me the telephone," said von Braun.

He spoke in German for a moment. There was no reading his face, but when he handed back the phone he said, "I go along."

"Thank you for dinner and all, Captain," Alex said politely as they got into the launch. "And please tell the contractor thank you for the binoculars."

The captain said nothing, sighing and shaking his head as he turned away.

"How come the new rocket is so small?" Chuck asked von Braun as they rode in the boat. "The V-2 with you and Ebbs in the picture is bigger."

"A lot of space in the V-2 was for the fuel," von Braun explained, "alcohol and the oxidizer. This one runs on something new. Its range is less, but the payload—that's the big thing—it is almost the same."

"What's payload?" Alex asked.

"The weight of the bomb in the nose," von Braun

193

replied, "or, better, what may someday be your space travel capsule, Astronaut Alexis. So now you two have classified information," he said with a strange smile, "so if the spies get you and torture you, you'll have to tell them what I just told you. But they won't bother. Do you know why? Because they already know," he said, glancing in the direction of the FBI men, who were listening as hard as they could.

"The milk-and-egg lady who comes over to Wallops every other day," von Braun explained, "she's in their pay, as are ten or twelve other people on Chincoteague."

Chuck let out a silent whistle of amazement as he caught Alex's eye.

A government car met the FBI launch. Minutes later, the five federal agents accompanying Jeep, Alex, Chuck, and von Braun showed up at Jester's Used Books.

Ebbs and Pete, along with TJ and his mother, were waiting outside. Ebbs opened the car door for her old friend.

"He said you sent them," von Braun said as he climbed out.

"*Absolutely not!*" Ebbs said, glaring at Chuck. "I wrote you about him, but this, he—and Alex—did all on their own. I didn't even know you'd be there."

Von Braun looked at Alex and nodded. "Astronaut Alexis is a most intrepid young lady," he said. "So now,

Captain Ebbs, explain how it is we get to rendezvous here tonight. I have heard their account; now I want to hear yours."

Ebbs described their trip down the Potomac and out to Tangier. "After lunch they took off to explore the island," she continued. "When I heard the *Captain Sam*'s whistle and they weren't around, I figured what they'd done, so my friend Pete and I hustled over to the mainland and started looking for them. No trouble tracking them: 'Older boy and his sister with a brown dog? Yeah, I seed 'em, watched 'em hitching,' the candy and sundries–store lady told us. 'Jester boy picked 'em up in his tomato truck.' We went to the Jesters' and met the boy—that's him over there—and he took us out to where he'd dropped them. Nothing to see there. On the way back we stopped at Cousin Marge's café. Right off Marge began to blow: 'Oh, they was here all right. Fed their dog on the floor, didn't leave no tip, and then they stoled Mr. Brownlowe's boat. De-linquents!'

"There was nothing for us to do but come back here to the Jesters' and wait—and watch. There's no civilian telephoning out there. I figured Alex would get them back here safe sooner or later."

Alex rocked back a little hearing that, but she knew it was true.

"We saw the sky light up," Ebbs continued, "then

your rocket went streaking across like a white-hot pencil. What seemed a long time later we heard the roar. The Jester boy told us he'd invited them to dinner—and here they are."

"*Ach!*" Von Braun snorted.

The agents started to leave.

"No," said von Braun. "Wait here. In a few minutes you must take me back."

The chief gave him a sour look.

As everybody moved toward the bookshop door, TJ cornered his new friends.

"You got on Wallops and stood there where they did the launch, then got the FBI to haul you back here in army clothes with no jail or fine or nothing, and they gave you those binoculars?" he whispered, shaking his head. "Wow!"

"Chuck saved the launch," Alex said. "It wouldn't have gone up if he hadn't told them how to fix it."

Once they were all inside, von Braun turned to Ebbs. "What are you going to do with these two? She has school she must finish," he said, pointing to Alex. "But Charles—what do you do with him?"

"Let me work for you," Chuck said. "Give me a job."

Von Braun pursed his lips. "Why did you do this?" he asked, almost as if he hadn't heard.

Chuck took a deep breath. "Because during the war

we hid in the basement shelter from what you were going to drop on us like you did to London. I wanted to be able to see what was coming—see better than what the searchlights could pick up. When I started learning about radar I figured that was it. I came here because I wanted to see the dishes, see how they worked, see the rockets you're making."

He stopped, his face flushed. Alex and Jeep stood tensed.

Von Braun took it in unblinking.

"You are a boy with clever hands," he said finally. "During the war we hear stories about boys like you. If an American jeep breaks, the driver jumps out and tinkers around until he fixes it, sometimes with something he makes out of what he's got in his pocket or a bit of wire or a tin can he finds by the road.

"With us, it is different, or it was. Work was done by class. The driver was of a higher class than the mechanic, so when his machine failed someone from the repair depot was summoned. I was often scolded by my superiors for getting my hands dirty.

"Your American rocket genius—Goddard—he was a tinkerer too, but he was also professor of physics. You, Charles, you are just a tinkerer, no?"

Chuck stared at him.

"You have talent I can use," von Braun continued

slowly, thoughtfully, "an inventor's energy, but what about your schooling? Ebbs says you are not technically trained beyond what you have taught yourself about radio. With us, every person on the shop floor must be able to read plans and do calculations. Nothing ever gets built exactly to plan. You have to be able to do the math to make things fit.

"You are ignorant and you are dangerous. You would tickle the porcupine—never mind the danger to yourself, but what about everyone around? What about her?" he asked, pointing to Alex.

"A fearless man is a more dangerous comrade than a coward," he said grimly. "You have scars, but you have not learned the lessons of those scars. Sneaking onto Wallops—you could have got shot, you and Alexis too, yes? And then what next gets into your head?"

Alex could see the muscles working in Chuck's face.

"Give me my chance and you'll see," Chuck said in a strangled voice. "I'll prove myself. You need me. I don't have to read plans. I can figure things out on my own. I can fix things, find stuff for you, and then you can send me up in the man-carrying rocket I've been reading about."

"What if you crashed or couldn't bail out, just kept going?" von Braun asked.

"That's OK," Chuck said eagerly. "Especially the keeping going part. I'd get to see it all!"

Alex caught her breath. It was like what she remembered from Captain Smith: *I wanted to get out of bounds, escape the gravity of the known world.*

"It is the answer I expected from you," von Braun said after a pause. "You are impulsive, reckless. It is a virtue in this work to be hungry for risks—they are everywhere. You cannot teach someone that hunger; it is like telling a timid man how to cross the river on a narrow log. He takes one step and falls in, while the reckless one skips across. But you need the discipline of training, Charles, and the discipline of restraint. With you it is all living on the edge, everything made up as you go along, test after test for the thrill of it—climbing towers, stealing airplanes, sneaking into the highest-security zone. Real work does not burn so hot, so fast. How can you slow yourself down?"

Alex watched to see what Chuck would say. He didn't say anything.

"Let me see if I can get him ready for you," Ebbs said quietly. "He reminds me of the young German rocketeer I heard about who borrowed airplanes as a teenager and went all over looking into things he was not supposed to see. His father could do nothing with him—they hardly spoke—but then someone took him in hand and turned him around. Perhaps you could do as much for this one."

Von Braun smiled grimly. "We will talk," he said.

"He can do anything," Alex said. "Anything! Just show him and watch!"

Von Braun shook his head. "Alexis, there is a big difference between his doing *anything*—the anything that comes into his head—and his doing the *something* I need done, which he would probably find boring after his experiences so far. Can you—can anyone—make him do only what he is ordered? Anyway, now I must go back and face those who will hold me responsible for this breach of security. There are many who would like to see me far away from their rocket projects. In Germany I never had such a thing happen—but I had no Charles there either."

He stood at the door. "I make no promises, Captain Ebbs. We will talk later. Now I must go back before I lose my Cinderella coachmen and their lovely yacht," he said, pointing to the FBI men.

To Alex they looked like they'd been eating lemons.

26

TJ

TJ's mother made an omelet with a lot of tomatoes and onions. They all sat around her kitchen table and listened to Chuck and Alex tell about sneaking onto Wallops.

Jeep barked frantically when Alex jumped up and started marching and singing again to show what they'd done. He'd had enough.

"You two are just plum lucky you didn't get shot," Mrs. Jester opined. "From all we hear, folks out there are real touchy, but then you don't exactly look like spies, and I reckon they was too busy to notice much, getting ready for the launch. Guess you brought 'em luck—the last three fizzled."

Chuck smiled. "I told VB how to fix the rocket."

"Go on!" TJ said, laughing.

"It's true," Alex said. "Chuck told him to cut the line

201

while the rocket sat live on the launchpad, and VB said he'd been thinking the same thing, so that's what they did."

TJ's mother made up beds for Pete and Ebbs. She got out stuff for Chuck and Alex to sleep on the floor in TJ's room.

"Oh no, no dogs," she said when Alex asked for some rags for Jeep. "Lie down with dogs, get up with fleas."

"Then I'm sleeping outside with him," Alex announced. Mrs. Jester relented.

Alex didn't stir until she smelled coffee and bacon. Only after she'd pushed all the bedding aside did Jeep move, starting with a languid rolling-over. A great shake followed to clear himself of fleas.

Over breakfast Alex got Ebbs to tell TJ about the T she'd described in her version of Smith's journal. Ebbs agreed that Alex's new friend looked a lot like the boy standing beside Smith in the portrait.

After TJ did his tomato run, with Alex helping, TJ took her to see the headstone. It was weathered and lichened over. Alex thought if you didn't know what you were looking for, it would look like an ordinary stone. The only singular thing about it was how it sort of stood up on end. She couldn't make out anything until TJ took her hand and guided her finger along the outline of the letter.

"Oh yeah!" she said.

After they got back to the bookshop, Ebbs said TJ should come up and see Smith's portrait as soon as tomato-hauling season was over. She said she'd cover his bus fare and put him up, seeing as how he was likely close to being kin.

"There's no point our going back to Tangier," she said. "Pete will take the *Captain Sam* over. Between Thanksgiving and Christmas we'll sail the *No Name* back up to Washington. What's important now is getting Chuck in a program for VB, so tomorrow morning we'll catch the bus home."

It was a little tricky getting Jeep on the bus. Company policy didn't allow for pets, just service animals, but Chuck made up some story about Jeep's name and his war service, so they got him aboard.

"*Focus* is the big thing," Ebbs told Chuck as they rode north.

"He's focused when I read aloud to him," Alex said. "He doesn't have any problem following then. Maybe if you taught him by talking to him it would work."

Ebbs looked thoughtful. "Worth a try," she said.

Alex listened, half dozing, as Chuck and Ebbs talked over their plans. The land outside the bus window flashed by like sheets of colored paper, flat field after flat field, soybeans and corn, sometimes alfalfa, an occasional grain silo, now and then a long chicken shed. Ebbs's attention was on Chuck now, but it didn't bother Alex as it had before. *She's getting him going, saving him,* she thought, counting the telephone poles. *I figured he'd take her over, but she's taking him over. It's not all on me anymore. And TJ's coming!*

"We're going to start with your writing," Ebbs was saying. "Benjamin Franklin learned to be a good writer because he had to write real slow as he set type in his print shop, one letter at a time. You don't jump around in your head doing that, so our program for you is going to be Franklin's making one letter at a time."

They ate the bag lunches Mrs. Jester had prepared as they skirted water, a finger of the bay Alex remembered from studying the maps. But she didn't want to check with Ebbs and interrupt her telling Chuck about the program. Alex saw possibilities for herself if she could attend some of the sessions.

"For math we're gonna start with the basics," Ebbs was saying. "I've got a box of sugar cubes we're going to work with, so you can see and feel what we're doing as we stack them and move 'em around, adding, dividing, multiplying. Then we'll cut a strip of paper into like pieces—fractions. You're going to see right off how numbers fit together—that they're really all just bits and pieces you can see and move around. You said with radio if you can see it you can do it. It'll be the same with math."

Chuck looked dubious.

"You're gonna like it," Ebbs insisted. "I'm going to get the music of math into your head. It's all rhythm, getting the numbers to dance. They want to dance. Once you start hearing their music you'll be charmed. First thing in the morning for half an hour before I go to work you're going to come up to my house for a talking math lesson like Alex suggested. Then when I get home we'll do a half-hour talking review. In between times, you're going to go to that new vocational school in town. I called. You're enrolled: an early Christmas present!"

"Holy cow, Ebbs!"

"Hold on," she said. "I'm not done yet. You know why they hang the carrot in front of the donkey's nose?"

"Yeah, to keep him going."

"That's part of it. The other part is to keep him from snatching at grass by the side of the road—getting diverted." She paused.

"So what's my carrot?" Chuck asked.

"Flight lessons. Saturdays we'll go out to the field at Rockville. A friend of mine from Paperclip days has an old Piper Cub—the two-seater J-type they trained army pilots on during the war. You do your part during the week—with no escapades—you get a carrot. Deal?"

"Deal!" said Chuck.

"What about me?" Alex demanded. "There's gotta be something in all this for me."

"Like what?" Ebbs asked.

"Flight lessons."

"They don't do them for kids," Chuck said.

"I'm not a kid anymore," Alex said, glowering. "I'm an astronaut in training. VB said so."

"I'll talk to my friend," Ebbs said. "We'll work out something."

That night, at home around the dinner table, Chuck asked, "Why is she doing all this for us?"

"Because you and Alex have become her family," Stuart replied. "She loves you."

Chuck started going up to Ebbs's every morning for Focus and Drill and every afternoon for review. He told Alex how Ebbs was talking him through numbers and holding his hand to shape his letters. Alex felt left out. Ebbs had no time for her now, and she and Chuck spent less and less time in the Moon Station. Alex saw what was coming.

The big consolation was that every Saturday she went with Ebbs and Chuck out to Rockville for a flying lesson. She had to sit on a pillow to manage the controls, and she couldn't solo, but she was learning to fly. The instructor said there was no question about it, she'd get her junior license the day she turned fourteen. *Just like VB,* Alex thought.

A week before Labor Day, Ebbs sent TJ money for a bus ticket to Washington. She took off work so she and Alex could meet his bus and drive him around Washington, showing him the Capitol high on its hill, the White House sitting in its great expanse of green lawn, the Lincoln Memorial out by the river. TJ was handsomer than Alex had remembered, and taller. He limped a little. "New shoes," he explained when Alex asked why. "Mom made me get 'em."

The thing he most wanted to see was the Moon Station, so as soon as they got to Alex's, she sent him up the slats. He almost fell when the screecher went off. That weekend TJ and Alex spent most of their time up there. Jeep insisted on going up with them. After being on the *No Name,* he was steady on his feet in the Station now.

By Christmas, Chuck was beginning to manage the basic design diagrams and calculations at the vocational school, and now even John could read what he wrote in blocky capital letters. Their parents invited Ebbs for Christmas dinner. She came with a letter. "Just came this afternoon, Special Delivery!" she announced. "VB's agreed to give Chuck a chance. He says they've got a school at Fort

Bliss that can pick up from where he is in his vocational schoolwork. If Chuck will enlist in the army and passes all their tests—which I'm sure he can do—VB will take him."

"Hey! Hurray!" Alex shouted, even as she fought to hold herself in.

In order to enlist, Chuck had to present a copy of his birth certificate. Stuart stopped at the bank on the way home from work to get it out of the safe-deposit box. He arrived home with two stamped documents. The whole family stood around when Chuck unfolded the top paper. It was in German. The only word Alex recognized was "Carlus." The names and surnames for both *Mutter* and *Vater*—mother and father—were strange.

Chuck's face twisted. "I knew it," he whispered.

"What does it mean?" Alex asked.

Her mother took a deep breath and explained. "After I came home and married your father I heard from a cousin in Germany about an infant whose parents—her dearest friends—had both just died in a typhus outbreak. My cousin could not keep this child. She begged me to come and take him. Germany was in chaos then, close to revolution, so we went and collected him. That second paper is the important one, Charles. It's your adoption certificate. There you see your full name: Charles Stuart Hart."

"I knew it," Chuck said again. Alex couldn't tell whether he was sad or angry.

"You knew from what I told you when I gave you the ring," his mother said. "When I gave it to you I said it was old and had come down to you from your family in Europe. I hinted and waited for you to ask, but you didn't. It seemed to me you didn't want to know more right then."

Chuck shook his head.

"You're the same brother I had yesterday," Alex said. "It's not like they just hung a name on you like you told TJ. They rescued you because they wanted you—they wanted you to make it, like Ebbs and VB and me."

"And me!" John said.

A week later the whole family and Jeep and Ebbs stood together in Washington's huge Union Station. It was the biggest building Alex had ever been in, the waiting room an immense white marble hall with vaulted ceilings. Alex felt small in it. The government had sent Chuck a travel voucher to Fort Bliss with meals and everything provided. He seemed changed—serious, older, a little frightened. His chin-out, dare-'em edginess was gone. Alex had never seen him like that. It was like he'd settled into himself, wasn't fighting to get out. It was like after trying on all sorts of different lives he'd finally found the one that fit.

His train was announced. They went to the platform.

There were hugs all around. John gave Chuck an envelope. "It's the money I got tutoring Alex," he explained. "Good luck."

When Chuck got to Alex, he whispered, "Don't worry, Alley. I'm going to do it right this time. I'm going to do it right for both of us. You'll see."

"Yes," Alex said, clenching her teeth to keep from crying.

"Chin up, Alex," Ebbs ordered as they rode home together. "We've got work to do. Starting now, we're going to train you to be the astronaut VB said you'd be, get you ready for your Columbian moment."

"My what?" Alex asked, blinking back tears.

"You're gonna go off like Christopher Columbus," Ebbs said. "Up and away—like his setting-out orders: 'Nothing to the north, nothing to the south, nothing to the east'—only for you it's nothing to the west either—just *up*! Right?"

"Right," said Alex with a smile. She caught herself. *"Right!"*

ACKNOWLEDGMENTS

Kate Klimo, who had the idea of my telling this story; Martha Armstrong, who knew them; and Dr. Jane Cotton Ebbs, who got me started when I was ten with talk about her space-food work for the army.

Others who helped: Arlene and Barry Borden, Abigail and Alan Dallmann, David Rohn, Jonathan Flaccus, Faith Moeckel, Martin Levitt, Jeffrey Carr, Robert Herbert, Dawn Armstrong, and Dr. Peter H. Smith, senior research scientist and principal investigator for the Mars Phoenix Lander, of the Lunar and Planetary Laboratory at the University of Arizona. "We're bound to find *something* out there!" he said when I interviewed him.

Suggestions for further reading: Karen Ordahl Kupperman's *Captain John Smith* (Chapel Hill: University of North Carolina Press, 1988) is a good collection of John Smith's writings. Another is John Lankford's *Captain John Smith's America* (New York: Harper & Row, 1967). For more about Wernher von Braun, I recommend

Michael J. Neufeld's *Von Braun: Dreamer of Space, Engineer of War* (New York: Knopf, 2007) and Ernst Stuhlinger and Frederick I. Ordway III's *Wernher von Braun: Crusader for Space* (Florida: Krieger Publishing Company, 1994).